He cleared [...] **what we need to do."**

"It is? And who's this *we*?"

"Me and you. We need to figure out why you were snatched in the first place and what it has to do with Denver." He rubbed his hands together, the thought of being with Sue, of working beside Sue, making his blood sing.

"I don't think so, Mancini."

"What? Why? Major Denver's life might depend on it, not to mention your safety."

"You and me working together? Spending days and nights together? Heads together?"

"Yeah." He couldn't stop his mouth watering at the prospect, especially when she put it like that.

"We both know that's a prescription for disaster."

"Why is that?" He folded his arms and braced a shoulder against the window, knowing damn well why she thought his idea stank but wanting to hear it from her lips.

"I... We..." Her cheeks sported two red flags.

He'd never seen Sue flustered before. Could he help it if it gave him a prick of satisfaction?

UNDERCOVER ACCOMPLICE

Carol Ericson

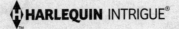

Recycling programs
for this product may
not exist in your area.

ISBN-13: 978-1-335-60476-7

Undercover Accomplice

Copyright © 2019 by Carol Ericson

This edition published by arrangement with Harlequin Books S.A.

For questions and comments about the quality of this book, please contact us at CustomerService@Harlequin.com.

Printed in U.S.A.

Carol Ericson is a bestselling, award-winning author of more than forty books. She has an eerie fascination for true-crime stories, a love of film noir and a weakness for reality TV, all of which fuel her imagination to create her own tales of murder, mayhem and mystery. To find out more about Carol and her current projects, please visit her website at www.carolericson.com, "where romance flirts with danger."

Visit the Author Profile page at Harlequin.com.

CAST OF CHARACTERS

Sue Chandler—This CIA agent has so many secrets she can't keep them straight, but if she hopes to save her reputation and her life, she'll have to come clean to the one man who can save both...even if it destroys him.

Hunter Mancini—A Delta Force soldier out to clear his commander's name, he doesn't have to be asked twice to check into the kidnapping story of a CIA agent he shared a sizzling fling with in Paris. Now that agent is in trouble, but he can't help her if she won't tell him her secrets...and one is sure to rock his world.

Drake Chandler—The unplanned child of his mother's affair with a Delta Force soldier, he has to be kept under wraps for his own safety.

The Falcon—A CIA black ops agent so undercover his own government doesn't know who he is.

Major Rex Denver—Framed for working with a terrorist group, the Delta Force commander has gone AWOL and is on the run, but he knows he's onto a larger plot and knows he can count on his squad to have his back and help clear his name.

Prologue

He ducked into the cave and swept the beam from the weak flashlight around the small space. Releasing a frosty breath, he slid down the wall of the cave into a crouch and faced the entrance, balancing his weapon on his knees.

After he'd helped Rafi and the others fight off the intruders who'd attacked their village, he took off for the hills—but not before he'd arranged another meeting with Pazir.

The last time he'd tried to meet with Pazir, it had led to the death of an army ranger, the possible death of one of his Delta Force team members and his own decision to go AWOL. He hoped for a better result this time.

A bush outside the cave rustled and he coiled his thigh muscles, getting ready to spring. His trigger finger twitched.

A harsh whisper echoed in the darkness. "Denver? Major Denver?"

He rose slowly, his jacket scraping the wall of the cave, the light from his flashlight illuminating a figure on hands and knees at the cave's entrance. "If you have any weapons, toss them in first. If you're not alone...you soon will be."

Pazir sat back on his heels and tossed a small pistol onto the dirt floor. He rummaged through the clothes on his body and flicked a knife through the air. It landed point down on the ground.

"That's all I have." Pazir continued forward on his knees, his hands in the air. "I had nothing to do with the ambush at our previous meeting. I barely got out of there with my life."

"The other Delta Force soldier? Asher Knight? Do you know what happened to him?"

"He survived."

Denver almost sank to the dirt again as relief coursed through his rigid muscles. "You know that for sure?"

"I know that he and the others are challenging the story that's out there about you."

"They are?" Denver's spine stiffened, and he lined it up against the cave wall again.

"Your men are loyal to you, Denver."

"But they haven't cleared me yet?"

"They're getting close. My sources tell me there's a battle raging about your guilt in the highest levels of government."

"You have good sources, Pazir." Denver gestured with his weapon. "Sit. What else have they told you? What do you know about those weapons at the embassy outpost in Nigeria? What do you know about the car bomb at the Syrian refugee camp?"

"Al Tariq."

Denver cleared his throat and spit. "Too small. I know that group and there's no way they could pull off what they're doing."

"They're the front group in the region. They're being used to do some of the grunt work. They're being used to track you down."

"By whom? Who's behind this and what do they want?"

"As far as I know, it's an international group, moles from different government agencies working together. They want weapons, and they're close to getting their hands on a nuclear device."

Denver swore, finally loosening the grip on his weapon. "That's what I was afraid of, and now you've just confirmed it."

"Has to be more than a rumor, Denver."

"I wanna know who's at the top. It's not good enough to finger Al Tariq."

Pazir scratched his beard and squatted across from Denver. "I know Al Tariq wasn't responsible for kidnapping that CIA agent."

"That female?"

"She was getting too close to the truth—just like you."

"They released her."

"She escaped."

"And you think the people who kidnapped Agent Chandler are the same ones pulling the strings for Al Tariq and trying to get their hands on this nuclear device?"

"I know it, Denver. Don't ask me how."

"Then I need to figure out who kidnapped Chandler."

"From here?" Pazir threw out one arm.

"I have to stay in hiding. You don't."

Pazir snorted. "I can't exactly run around the globe and travel to Washington, either."

"No, but you can get a message out for me, can't you?"

"Yes." Pazir reached into his pouch and pulled out a piece of flatbread. He ripped it in half and thrust one piece at Denver. "You want me to try to send a message to Agent Chandler?"

"I want you to send a message to one of my Delta Force team members. Hunter Mancini worked with Chandler on a covert mission once, and they got… close. You get a message to Mancini, and he can contact Chandler. Maybe she has some insight into who held her and what she was working on, but she's afraid to say anything."

"I can do that." Pazir pulled a pencil and pad of paper from his bag. "Give me the details."

As Denver chewed through the rough bread, he rattled off instructions to Pazir for contacting Mancini. "I don't have to tell you not to let this fall into the wrong hands."

"I give up nothing."

"Shh." Denver sidled along the wall of the cave and peered out the entrance. "We're not alone."

Pazir lunged for his weapon. "We'll fight them off together."

"You go." Denver grabbed a handful of Pazir's jacket. "I'll distract them. Get that message to Mancini if it's the last thing you do."

Chapter One

Sue slipped the burner phone from the inside pocket of her purse. She swiped a trickle of sweat from her temple as she reread the text and ducked into the last stall in the airport bathroom. Her heart fluttered in her chest just like it always did before she made a call to The Falcon.

He answered after one ring. "Seven, one, six, six, nine."

The numbers clicked in her brain and she responded. "Ten, five, seven, two, eight."

"Are you secure?"

The altered voice grated against her ear as she peeked through the gap between the stall door and its frame at several women washing their hands, scolding children, and wheeling their bags in and out of the bathroom, too concerned with their own lives to worry about someone reciting numbers on a cell phone.

Their nice, normal lives.

"Yeah."

"You got the name of the barbershop wrong. There's no Walid there."

"That's not possible."

"You misheard the name…or they purposely fed you the wrong one because they made you."

Sue swallowed and pressed her forehead against the cool metal door. "They didn't."

"Because they would've killed you when you were with them?"

"That's right." Sue yanked off a length of toilet paper from the roll and stepped in front of the toilet to make it flush automatically. "I've been doing this for a while. I'd know."

"That's what I like about you, Nightingale. You're a pro. You've already proven you'll do anything for the cause."

She swallowed the lump in her throat and sniffed. "Next move?"

"We need the correct barbershop."

"I can't exactly call up my contact and ask him."

"You'll figure it out. Like I said, you're a pro."

The Falcon ended the call before she could respond.

Sighing, she pushed out of the stall and washed her hands. On her way out of the bathroom, she almost bumped into her stepmother.

"Where have you been? We need to get to our gate. I can't wait to get out of this place. I hate D.C."

Sue dropped to her knees in front of her son, regretting that she'd spent their last precious minutes together on the phone with The Falcon—regretting so much more. She grabbed Drake's hands and kissed the tips of his sticky fingers, inhaling the scent of cinnamon that clung to his skin. "Be a good boy for Gran on the airplane."

Drake batted his dark eyelashes. "You go airplane, too, Mama?"

"No, cupcake. Just you and Gran this time, but I'll visit you soon."

Linda fluttered a tissue between the two of them. "Wipe your hands, Drake."

"That's not going to help, Linda. He had a cinnamon roll for breakfast. He's going to have to wash his hands in the restroom." Sue waved her hand behind her at the ladies' room.

Pursing her lips, Linda snatched back the tissue. "Cinnamon rolls for breakfast? You spoil him when he's here. I'll get him a proper lunch once we get through security, if he still has any appetite left."

He will unless you ruin it.

Sue managed to eke out a smile, as Drake was watching her with wide eyes. "Nothing spoils Drake's appetite. He could eat a horse and ask for dessert."

"We don't eat horses, Mama." Drake giggled and Sue pinched the end of his nose. "Give me another hug."

Drake curled his chubby arms around her neck, and Sue pressed her tingling nose against his hair. "Love you, cupcake."

"Love you." Drake smacked his lips against her cheek. "Can I live here?"

"Not yet, my lovey, but soon." Blinking the tears from her eyes, Sue straightened up and placed Drake's hand in her stepmother's. "Give my love to Dad."

Linda sniffed as she yanked up the handle of her suitcase. "I don't know why some people have children if they can't be bothered to take care of them."

"Linda." Sue ducked toward her stepmother and said through clenched teeth, "I told you. This…arrangement won't be forever, and I don't appreciate your talking like that in front of my son."

Linda's pale eyes widened a fraction and she backed up. "I hope you're not going to be landing in trouble every other month, or you'll never have Drake with you. You were right to leave him with your sister. Children need stability. You should give up this crazy job and find yourself a husband to take care of you, a father for Drake, and settle down like your sister."

Sue opened her mouth and then snapped it shut. She'd promised herself not to argue with Linda—besides, her stepmother had a point. As it stood now, Sue couldn't keep her son with her and raise him properly—even if The Falcon had allowed it.

And he hadn't.

"It won't always be like this. I plan to transfer to another position, and then I can have him with me all the time. I'll contact you tonight for some face-to-face with Drake. Ask Dad. He knows how to do it."

"I know, I know. Your father knows everything."

"Thanks, Linda. Safe travels." Sue blew a kiss

to Drake as her stepmother hustled him toward the line for security.

She waved until they got to the front of the line. Knowing her father would be stationed at the airport in South Carolina to pick them up was the only thing that allowed her to turn away and leave the airport. Drake lived with her sister, Amelia, and her family, but they were in the Bahamas and Sue hadn't wanted Drake to go along, so she sent him to Dad and Linda.

Linda could take care of Drake's physical needs and keep him safe, but she trusted only Dad to meet Drake's emotional needs. Her stepmother didn't have the capacity for that job, as Sue suspected she trash-talked her to Drake whenever she got the chance.

If Sue had one more incident like the one she'd faced in Istanbul, she had no doubt her stepmother would move against her to take Drake away from her completely and declare her an unfit mother.

Sue clenched her teeth and exited the airport. She'd just have to make sure she didn't have any more of those close calls.

After she fed her parking receipt into the machine and the arm lifted, Sue flexed her fingers on the steering wheel of the car and glanced in her rearview mirror. With Drake's visit over, she could finally breathe…and find out who was following her. The possibilities were endless.

She navigated out of the airport and drove straight to her office. She had to confront her supervisor, Ned Tucker, about her suspicions. She'd already been debriefed after the kidnapping. Why was the CIA still dogging her? And if it wasn't the CIA, maybe Ned could help her figure out who it was. She hadn't wanted to tell The Falcon about this new development.

He thought she was a pro who could handle anything. She could, but handling everything on her own all the time had gotten old. Sometimes a girl just needed a shoulder to lean on. She'd had that shoulder...once.

She rolled up to the parking gate of the office and held her badge out the window.

The security guard waved her through, and she parked her car. Slipping her badge lanyard over her head, she marched toward her office building. She'd taken the day off to drop off Drake and Linda at the airport, but she couldn't wait any longer to get to the bottom of this mystery tail.

She punched the elevator button and almost bumped into one of her coworkers coming out.

Peter held up his hands. "Whoa, what's the hurry?"

"Sorry, Peter." She stepped to the side.

"Thought you were out today."

"Half day. I need to talk to Ned."

"I think he needs to talk to you, too."

"Why? Was he looking for me? He knows I'm out today."

Peter shrugged. "You might wanna turn around and go home."

"Why?"

Peter pivoted away from her and called over his shoulder, "Take someone's advice for once, Sue."

If Peter thought his cryptic warning would send

her home, he didn't know her very well. She dropped her hand from holding open the elevator doors and stepped inside.

Good. If Ned wanted to talk to her, maybe he wanted to explain what the hell was going on.

The elevator deposited her onto the fifth floor, and she badged the door to the cubicles. The hum of low voices and keyboard clicks created a comforting welcome.

As she turned the corner to her row, she stumbled to a stop. A man she didn't know was hanging on to the corner of her cube and Ned's head bobbed above the top.

She bit the inside of her cheek and continued walking forward.

At her approach the stranger turned, and his eyes widened. "Chandler."

She stopped at the entrance to her cubicle, her gaze darting from Ned to a woman sitting at her desk, accessing her computer.

"Wh-what's going on here, Ned?"

Her boss ran a hand over his bald head, his forehead glistening with sweat. "I thought you were out today, Sue."

"So, what? You figured you and a couple of strangers could get into my computer in my absence?"

The guy to her right straightened up and pulled back his shoulders. "Ms. Chandler, we've noticed some irregularities on your workstation."

"Irregularities?" She shot a look at Ned, who refused to meet her gaze. "I don't understand."

The woman sitting in front of her computer twisted her head around, a tight smile on her face. "I found another one."

"Another one what?" Sue stepped into her cube, hovering over the woman seated at her desk.

The man placed a hand on Sue's arm. "Perhaps it's best we talk in Ned's office."

Sue had noticed a few heads popping up from other cubicles. She lifted her own chin. She knew damn well she didn't have any irregularities on her computer. The Falcon would make sure of that—unless these were communiqués from him.

"Let's go, then." She shook off the man's hand and charged out of her cubicle and down the aisle to Ned's office in the corner.

She reached Ned's office before the two strangers, with Ned right behind her. She swung around, nearly colliding with him. "What's going on, Ned?"

"They received an anonymous tip about you forwarding classified emails and documents to your home computer."

"What? You know I'd never do anything like that. I've been in the field myself. There's no way I'd put anyone in danger."

"I know that, Sue." His gaze darted over his shoulder, and then he sealed his lips as the two investigators approached.

Sue shuffled into the room as Ned sat down behind his desk. "Take a seat, Sue."

"That's okay. I'll stand." Folding her arms, she squared her shoulders against the wall.

The two investigators remained standing, too.

The woman thrust out her hand, all business. "I'm Jackie Templeman."

Sue gripped her hand and squeezed hard, her lips twisting as Jackie blinked.

The man cleared his throat and dipped his head. "Robert Beall."

He didn't offer his hand and she didn't make a move to get it. She folded her arms across her chest and asked, "What did this anonymous email say?"

Templeman shot a glance at Ned. "To check your emails."

"You have no idea who sent it?"

"No." Templeman shook her head. "That's why it's anonymous."

Sue smirked. "Got it. So, you believe every anonymous email you receive and rush in to do an investigation?"

Templeman hugged her notebook to her chest, as if guarding state secrets. "Not everyone."

"Oh, I see." Sue shoved off the wall and plopped into the chair across from Ned. "Just the ones about me."

Beall finally found his voice. "Because of your… um…the incident."

"Funny thing about that incident." Sue drummed her fingers on Ned's desk. "You'd think the Agency would be kissing my…rear end, considering a leak on their part led to my kidnapping in the first place."

"And then you escaped." Templeman tilted her head.

"Yeah, another reason the Agency should be nominating me for a medal or something instead of combing through my computer."

"You escaped from a group of men holding you in Istanbul." Templeman's delicate eyebrows formed a V over her nose.

Sue snorted. "I guess that's hard for *some* people to believe, but *some* female agents aren't pencil-pushing computer geeks. Some of us know how to handle ourselves."

A smile tugged at Beall's lips, but he wiped it out with his hand.

"Besides, I was debriefed on that incident and the case was closed. You still seem to be using it to go after me."

"The point—" Templeman straightened her jacket "—is that we *did* find anomalies on your computer. Enough for us to confiscate your machine and suspend you."

"Suspend?" Sue jumped from the chair. "Is that true, Ned?"

"Just until they can figure out everything. I think there has to be a mistake, and I told them that. We already know those emails implicating Major Rex Denver and sent to a CIA translator were fakes. I'm confident that this investigation is going to find something similar with these emails and you'll be in the clear, Sue."

"Suspension starting now?"

"Yes, we'll accompany you back to your cubicle if you want to take any personal items with you." Templeman pushed past Beall and opened the door.

"I don't have anything there I need." Sue smacked her hand on Ned's desk. "Let me know when this is over, Ned."

"Of course, Sue. Don't worry."

As she stepped through the door, Templeman tapped her shoulder. "Badge."

Sue whipped the lanyard over her head and tossed it at Templeman's chest, but it slipped through the investigator's fingers and landed on the floor. The woman couldn't even make a good catch. No wonder she had a hard time believing Sue had escaped her captors.

Sue strode out of the office, not looking right or left. When she stepped out onto the sidewalk, she took a deep breath of fresh air.

Maybe she sent her son away early for nothing. Maybe her senses had been on high alert because the Agency *had* been tracking her. Now that they'd made their move and suspended her and confiscated her computer, they'd back off.

The thought didn't make her feel much better. The CIA didn't trust her, and being falsely accused made her blood boil. Of course, if the Agency knew about her work with The Falcon, the accusations might not be false. She didn't have to worry about that, though. The Falcon would have her covered.

As she waited for the elevator in the parking garage, her phone buzzed and she squinted at the text message from her friend, Dani Howard.

Dani knew she'd sent Drake back home and figured Sue needed some cheering up. Dani had no idea how much cheering up she needed.

Sue texted her friend back. I'm up for cocktails tonight.

What the hell did she have to lose at this point?

SUE SPOTTED DANI already sitting at the bar, and she squeezed between the people and the tall tables to reach her. "This the best you could do?"

Dani gave her a one-armed hug. "I just got here five minutes ago. Haven't even ordered a drink yet."

Hunching over the bar, Sue snapped her fingers and shouted, "Hey."

The bartender raised his hand. "Be right with you."

A minute later he took their order for two glasses of white wine.

Dani sighed as she flicked back her hair. "It must be your commanding presence that gets their attention. Did you see Drake off okay today?"

"I did." Sue rolled her eyes. "Of course, I had to put up with Linda's jabs."

"Our mothers should have a contest to see who can outshame the single moms." Dani picked out some pretzels from the bowl of snack mix on the bar and popped one into her mouth.

"Stepmother. At least Fiona's dad is in the picture."

"You say that like it's a good thing."

"Okay then, at least Fiona lives with you and you're not in constant fear of losing custody of her."

Dani folded back the corners of the napkin the bartender had tossed down when he took their order. "You know I'm planning to drive down to Savannah, and I'd be happy to drop in on Drake for you. Text me your parents' address, and I'll see if I can make the detour—just a familiar face from where Mom lives might make a big difference."

"That would be great, but I don't want to put you out."

"Happy to do it." Dani snatched their glasses from the bartender's hand and handed one to Sue. "Drink."

Sue took a big gulp of wine, but there wasn't enough alcohol in the world right now to drown her sorrows.

"Stop beating yourself up. You're saving the freakin' world." Dani tilted her head. "I suppose you can't tell me about this hush-hush assignment of yours."

Not only did she not have a hush-hush assignment, she didn't have any assignment—unless she counted the one to get the name of the right barbershop.

Sue put a finger to her lips and swirled her wine in the glass. "No questions about my job."

"Don't even ask about *my* job…except for the new resident who started his rotation." Dani winked.

"Not another doctor. You need to date outside the medical field."

"I need to date and I may have just found the answer to our prayers." Dani tilted her head to the side and twirled a strand of her red hair around one finger.

Sue put her glass to her lips and shifted her gaze above the rim toward a table to Dani's right, where two men had their heads together. "Are you sure they aren't gay?"

"Not the way they've been eyeing us for the past few minutes." Dani drew back her shoulders and puffed out her ample chest. "Besides, they have a table, and we're stuck here at the bar getting squeezed out."

One of the men had noticed Dani's move and he sat up, nudging his buddy.

An evening with Dani always ended in the company of men, and for once, Sue welcomed the distraction. She smiled at the eager suitors.

One of the guys raised his glass and pointed to the two empty chairs at their table.

"And score." Dani wiggled her fingers in the air. "I get the blond unless you have a preference. I'm just thinking about cute little strawberry-blond siblings for Fiona."

Sue's gaze shifted to the dark-haired man as she pushed away from the bar. At least he was her type. "Go for it, Dani."

The two men jumped from their seats and pulled

out the chairs for her and Dani. She and Dani did a little dance to get Dani seated next to the blond.

He spoke first. "You two looked so uncomfortable packed in at the bar. It seemed a shame to let these two chairs go to waste."

"Thank you. I'm Dani and this is Sue." Dani's southern accent always got more pronounced in front of men, and they seemed to eat it up.

Dani's future husband pointed to himself. "I'm Mason—" and then he pointed to his companion "—and this is Jeffrey."

They all said their hellos and launched into the inane small talk that characterized meet-ups in bars. Sue had no intention of winding up with Jeffrey or anyone else at the end of the evening and tried to keep her alcohol consumption to a minimum.

She failed.

Mason, or maybe it was Jeffrey, ordered a bottle of wine for the table, and then another. Although Sue continuously sipped from her glass, the liquid never dropped below the halfway point, and by the time she staggered to the ladies' room on her second trip, she realized the men had been topping off her wine.

She'd have to put a lid on that glass when she got back to the table.

As she wended her way through the crowded bar, she stumbled to a stop when she saw Jeffrey alone at the table. She clutched her small purse to her chest and took the last few steps on unsteady legs. "Where are Mason and Dani?"

"They left—together." Jeffrey lifted one shoulder.

Sue sank into the chair, snatching her phone from the side pocket on her purse. "Whose idea was that?"

"I think it was mutual." Jeffrey held up his hands. "Don't worry. I know we didn't hit it off like they did, and I have no expectations."

She scowled at him over the top of her phone. "I hope not."

Dani picked up on the first ring. "Hey, Sue, did Jeffrey tell you I left with Mason?"

"He did. Are you okay?"

"I'm fine." Dani giggled and sucked in a breath. "I'm sorry. I shouldn't have left you there with Jeffrey."

"That's okay. As long as you're all right. Do you have an address where you're going?"

"The Hay-Adams."

"Okay. Be careful."

Dani ended the call on another giggle and Sue shoved her phone back into her purse.

Jeffrey raised one eyebrow. "Your friend okay? Mason's a good guy."

"He'd better be." Sue raised her phone and snapped a picture of Jeffrey. "Just in case."

A spark of anger lit Jeffrey's eyes for a second, or maybe she'd imagined it. Then he tucked some bills beneath his empty glass. "Can I at least see you home?"

She shook her head and then clutched the edge of the table as a wave of dizziness engulfed her brain. She took a sip of water. "I'm fine, thanks."

"Really? You don't look fine. The booze was

flowing as fast as the conversation tonight. You look…woozy."

Woozy? Someone had stuffed a big cotton ball in her head to keep her brain from banging around. After the day she'd had, she'd wanted to let loose, tie one on. Now she had to face the consequences.

"I didn't drive. I can just hop on the Metro, one stop." She staggered to her feet and grabbed the back of her chair. She'd be paying for her overindulgence tomorrow morning for sure.

Jeffrey jumped from his chair. "Are you positive I can't help you? I can walk you to the station or call you a taxi or rideshare car."

She narrowed her eyes and peered at him through a fog. Why was he so insistent? Why didn't he just leave her alone?

She raised her hand and leveled a finger at him. "Stay right where you are."

Jeffrey cocked his head and a lock of his brown hair slipped free from the gel and made a comma on his wrinkled brow.

Had she made sense? She tried to form another word with her thick tongue, but she couldn't get it to cooperate.

She resorted to sign language, raising her middle finger. Would he get the picture now? "Whatever." He plopped back into his chair. "Just be careful."

She swung to the side, banging her hip on the corner of the table, jostling all the empties. Putting her head down, she made a beeline for the door.

Once outside, she gulped in breaths of the cold air

but couldn't seem to revive herself. Walking should help. She put one foot in front of the other and weaved down the sidewalk. Oncoming pedestrians gave her a wide berth, and a few made jokes.

Oh, God. Was she a joke? A drunk joke? She placed a hand flat against the side of a building and closed her eyes.

She hadn't been this drunk since college days, and she didn't intend to make the same stupid mistakes she'd made back then.

She shoved a hand into the pocket of her leather moto jacket and fumbled for her phone. Jeffrey had been right about one thing—she should call a taxi.

After she pulled the phone from her jacket, it slipped from her hand and bounced twice on the sidewalk before landing in the gutter.

She dropped to a crouch and stuck her hand over the curb to feel for the phone. The effort proved too much for her and she fell over onto her side.

Good thing her son couldn't see her now, passed out like a wino in the gutter.

She flexed her fingers toward her phone but lead weights had been attached to their tips—and her eyelids. DC Metro would pick her up and she'd lose her job for sure.

"Sue? Sue? You're coming with me now."

An arm curled around her shoulders and pulled her upright. Jeffrey. He'd followed her out to finish what he'd started.

She arched her back, but her gelatinous spine

sabotaged the act and she collapsed against Jeffrey's chest.

He had her.

"It's all right. I'm taking you to my hotel."

Her lips parted and she uttered a protest, but just like everything in her life lately, the situation had already spiraled out of her control.

Her mind screamed resistance, but her body had already succumbed.

SUE STRETCHED HER limbs and rubbed her eyes, the silky, soft sheets falling from her shoulders. Then the memories from the night before tumbled through her mind in a kaleidoscope of images.

She bolted upright against the king-size bed's headboard, yanking the sheets to her chin to cover her naked body.

Had Jeffrey raped and abandoned her at the hotel? Was his name even Jeffrey?

The bathroom door crashed open and a large man stopped cold on the threshold. "God, you look beautiful even after the night you had."

Sue's mouth dropped open as she took in the man at the bathroom door, towel hanging precariously low on a pair of slim hips.

The man she'd betrayed and who still haunted her dreams…and it sure as hell wasn't Jeffrey.

Chapter Two

The look on Sue's face shifted from shock to disbelief, to horror, to pain and to a whole bunch of other stuff he couldn't figure out. And that had been his problem with Sue Chandler all along—he'd never been able to figure her out.

Those luscious lips finally formed a word, just one. "You."

He spread his arms wide. "In the flesh. Did you expect me to leave you in the gutter, like you left me?"

"As I recall, it was a luxury hotel." She patted the pillow next to her. "Somewhat like this one—and all I did was check out."

"Details, details."

She pointed at him. "Your towel is slipping. Not interested in seeing that package—again."

The years hadn't softened Sue Chandler one bit. He held up one finger. "Give me a second."

As Sue turned her tight face away, he crossed the room to his suitcase, tugged a pair of briefs from an inside pocket, dropped his towel and pulled on his underwear.

"There." He turned toward the bed. "Decent."

Her gaze flicked over his body, making him hot and hard, as only Sue Chandler could do with one look from her dark eyes.

The twist of her lips told him she'd noticed the effect she had on him.

"Maybe not decent enough." He yanked open a dresser drawer and pulled out some jeans. He stepped into them, feeling less cocky under Sue's unrelenting stare, but he had the upper hand for once.

"Now, are you going to tell me what you were doing last night stumbling along the streets of DC close to midnight?"

"I live here." Her jaw hardened. "What are *you* doing here and how did you happen to find me?"

"You're not exactly hard to find. You work for the CIA and live in DC, and I knew you weren't on assignment, not after..."

"You know about my kidnapping?" She drew her knees to her chest beneath the sheets, clasping her arms around her legs.

"Several special forces knew about it and were actively planning your rescue." He tilted his head to the side. "But you didn't need rescuing."

"Don't go throwing any parades. The kidnappers were not that bright." She blinked. "Is that why you're here? Have you been following me?"

"Whoa, wait." He tossed his towel onto the foot of the bed. "I followed you from your place to the bar last night. That's it. I just arrived yesterday."

She sank back against the stacked pillows.

"Why'd you follow me? Are you here on official duty, or something? I've already been debriefed by the Agency."

"Official duty? Really? What would a Delta Force soldier have to do with the kidnapping of a CIA agent?"

"Don't try that 'Who, me?' stuff with me, Mancini. You didn't seek me out to profess your undying love. You had three years to do that—and not a peep."

He reached into the closet and jerked a shirt from a hanger, leaving it swinging wildly. "You're not gonna pin that on me. I got the message loud and clear that you were moving on. Did you expect me to chase after you?"

Sue opened her mouth and then snapped it shut. Then her eyes widened and she gathered the covers around her body. "I'm naked. How did I get naked?"

"I took your clothes off—sorry." He gestured to a pile of clothing in the corner of the room. "Yours were dirty. I didn't think it was sanitary to put you to bed in filthy clothes."

"How thoughtful." She snorted. "I fell on the sidewalk. I'm sure you could've brushed the dirt from my slacks and left my underwear alone."

He cleared his throat. "You vomited all over yourself when I got you to the room."

"Oh my God." She covered her mouth with both hands. "I don't know what happened last night. I—I apologize."

"Nothing I haven't handled hundreds of times before with my buddies. I'm sure we can send your clothes to the hotel's laundry or dry cleaning. I already cleaned off your boots and jacket."

"I don't know what to say. I'm embarrassed. I'm not sure what came over me. I did have a lot of wine last night, but I've never felt that way before."

"I'm thinking the fact that you upchucked saved you."

"Saved me from what?"

"Whatever was in your system."

"You mean besides the alcohol?" She twisted a lock of dark brown hair around her finger, not looking surprised at all. "What do you know? Why are you here in DC?"

He swallowed against his dry throat. He had to concentrate, but remembering Sue naked in bed had his thoughts scrambled.

Should he pretend he was here for her instead of trying to explain the real reason? He met those dark, shimmering eyes that seemed to see into his very soul. He couldn't lie to Sue—not that she'd believe him, anyway.

"I got a message from Major Denver."

"Major Rex Denver? AWOL Delta Force commander?"

"You know as well as I do that he isn't and never has been working with any terrorist organization against the US government. One of your own translators proved the emails she'd received implicating him were phony."

"I've heard all the stories, but if he's innocent,

why won't he come in? Why is he sending messages to you instead?"

"He doesn't feel it's safe yet. He's already been the victim of a setup, and he doesn't trust anyone."

"Yeah, I understand that." Sue bit her bottom lip. "What was the message? What are you supposed to do?"

"Contact you?"

"What? Why?"

"He believes the people who kidnapped you belong to the same group he's trying to bring down, the same group that he believes is planning some kind of spectacular attack."

Sue clenched the sheets in her fists. "Why does he think that?"

Hunter's pulse jumped. Again, no surprised looks from Sue. "Something his informant told him. Why? What happened during that kidnapping? Did they ever give you any reason why they snatched you?"

"Wait." She massaged her temple with two fingers. "I can't take all this in right now, especially not huddled under the covers with no clothes on. I need a shower. I need breakfast. I need clothes."

"The shower's all yours. I can send your clothes out to the laundry right now, if you're okay with eating room service wearing my sweats and T-shirt." He took a step to the side and slid open the closet door. He reached in, his hand closing around the fluffy terrycloth of a hotel robe. "You can wear this into the bathroom."

"Thanks."

She uttered the word between clenched teeth, almost grudgingly, but he'd take it at this point. Her reception of him had been chillier than he'd expected, especially since she was the one who had ended their brief affair by leaving him in his hotel room with no note, no phone call, no explanation.

He placed the robe across her lap, dropping it quickly and jerking back. Being close to Sue again had proven to be more difficult than he'd expected when he first got Denver's message. Undressing her last night and putting her to bed had been an exquisite torture. His hands lingering on her smooth flesh had screamed violation, so he'd made quick work of it.

"I'm going to bag your stuff and call housekeeping. I'll put a rush on it, so your clothes will be ready by the time we finish breakfast." He pinched the strap of her lacy bra between two fingers and held it up. "Anything need special attention or dry cleaning?"

"Everything is machine washable." She flicked her fingers in the air. "Turn around, please."

Not like he hadn't already seen every inch of her beautiful body.

"Yes, ma'am." He turned his back on her and stuffed her clothing into the hotel's plastic bag for laundry, as she rustled behind him.

She slammed the bathroom door before he even rose from the floor with her bag of clothing dangling from his fingertips.

Blowing out a breath, he wedged a shoulder

against the closet. He knew it wouldn't be easy reconnecting with Sue after what had happened in Paris, but she couldn't completely blame him for not contacting her, could she?

They'd met at a party of expats. He knew she was CIA, and she knew he was Delta Force on leave. They'd approached their relationship as a fling and had been enjoying each other's company until she'd turned cold. He'd assumed at the time it was because she knew they'd have to end their Paris idyll once he got deployed, even though he'd been ready to ask her to wait for him.

Maybe it hadn't been the wisest decision for him to get involved with someone so soon after separating from his wife, and maybe she got that vibe from him, although he hadn't gotten around to telling her about his wife. He hadn't wanted to open that can of worms until he'd gotten a signal from Sue that they had some kind of future. Once she'd shut that down, he'd shut down, too. He didn't need any more women in his life who couldn't accept his military career.

He pushed off the closet and grabbed the phone by the bed. He requested a laundry pickup and then room service, ordering eggs, bacon, the works. From what he'd seen of Sue's body last night, she still must work out and burn calories at a ferocious rate. With Sue's dedication to running, kickboxing and Krav Maga, he'd had no trouble imagining her escaping from a gaggle of hapless terrorists—even though others did.

He'd heard rumblings that Sue faked her kidnapping and miraculous escape but hadn't heard about any motive. Why would she fake a kidnapping in Istanbul? Glory? Sue wasn't like that. Didn't need that. The woman he'd met in Paris kept her head down and got to work. No nonsense. No drama.

And that's how she'd ended their affair.

The bathroom door swung open, and Sue poked her head into the room. "Can they do my clothes?"

"They haven't picked up yet, but they assured me they could have them ready by noon. Is that okay?" He glanced at the clock by the tousled bed. "You don't have to get to work?"

"I have a few days off. That's why I was out last night with my friend."

"When your friend left the bar with that guy, I thought maybe…" He shrugged.

"You thought I'd be leaving with someone, too?" She tucked a lock of wet hair beneath the towel wrapped around her head. "Queen of the one-night stands?"

"What we had wasn't…"

He choked to a stop as she sliced a hand through the air. "Don't want to discuss it."

"Housekeeping." The sharp rap at the door had him pivoting to answer it. He handed the bag to the woman. "I was told the clothes could be returned by noon."

"That's what I have on the order, sir."

By the time he turned back to the room, Sue had grabbed what she needed from his bag and retreated to the bathroom.

He ran a hand across his mouth. He didn't understand her anger at him. He hadn't been the one who abruptly left Paris without a word, without even a note on the pillow.

She'd hurt him more than he'd cared to admit, but he'd chalked it up to being dumped and accepted it as a sign that he shouldn't have gotten involved with someone so soon after Julia left.

Maybe Sue had expected him to run after her, pursue her, but he hadn't had the energy at that time for games and he'd let her go without a fight—clearly his loss.

She emerged from the bathroom again, yanking up the waistband of a pair of gray sweats that swam on her.

"I can turn up the thermostat in the room if you just wanna wear the big T-shirt."

"That's all right. I don't plan to run any marathons, or even leave the room."

The next knock on the door brought breakfast, and Hunter added a tip and signed the check. He lifted the cover on the first plate. "Eggs, bacon, hash browns. Is that okay?"

"Toast?"

"Under this one." He plucked a cover from a rack of toast. "Coffee?"

"Please."

She'd exchanged her ire for a cold civility. He couldn't decide which stung more. Over the years, he'd built up some ridiculous significance to their fling—Sue just set him straight.

He poured her a cup of coffee and nudged the cream and sugar toward her where she'd taken up a place across the table from him.

She dumped some cream into her coffee, picked up the cup and leveled a gaze at him over the rim. "Where did you sleep last night?"

His own coffee sloshed over the side of his cup. "The sofa."

"That small thing?"

"My legs hung over the edge, but I've had worse."

All the questions that must be bubbling in her brain and *that* one came to the surface first?

"Look, this is what happened." He slurped a sip of coffee for fortification. "I'd followed you to the bar from your place. I watched the entrance, waiting for you to come out, and I was going to approach you then."

"Why not sooner?"

"I told you, I'd just arrived in the afternoon, and I didn't have your address right away. Figured you'd be at work, anyway. By the time I got around to finding your place, you were on the move. I didn't want to interrupt your evening. I thought about leaving you a note, but…"

"You figured I might not contact you."

"So, I followed you to the bar and waited."

"How'd you know I was with Dani? A woman? You mentioned seeing my friend leave with a man."

He cleared his throat. "I went into the bar."

"You were watching me inside the bar?" She stabbed at her eggs with a fork. "Creepy."

His lips twitched. "Sorry. I didn't stay long. Then I waited outside and saw your friend leave."

"Just in time to see me staggering out."

"Scared the hell out of me."

"Why?"

"It didn't look…normal, and I knew you weren't a big drinker, or at least you weren't in Paris." There he was, acting like some big expert on Sue Chandler.

"It didn't *feel* normal." She dropped a half-eaten piece of toast onto her plate. "If that guy I was with, Jeffrey, drugged me, what did his friend do to Dani? And why would they want to do anything to either of us?"

"Before we try to answer that second question, why don't you give Dani a call?" He crumpled his napkin next to his plate and grabbed her phone off the charger. "I found your phone charger in your purse and took the liberty of hooking you up."

"Thanks. Seems like you thought of everything."

"Except that change of clothes." He dropped the phone into her palm.

While Sue called her friend, Hunter shook out his napkin and listened. Everything sounded okay on this end. Maybe he'd been wrong about Sue being in danger.

She ended the call and tapped the edge of the phone against her chin.

"Everything okay?"

"Dani's already home. Seems Mason was the perfect gentleman. She passed out in his hotel room, and he checked out before she woke up. He left her a note telling her to order anything she wanted from room service and to take her time. And she woke up with all her clothes on…which is more than I can say for myself."

"Maybe Dani passed out before she had a chance to hurl all over herself."

"Don't remind me." She made a face and stuck out her tongue.

"That's good, then. Dani is safe at home with her virginity intact."

Sue covered her lower face with her napkin and raised her eyebrows. "I wouldn't go that far."

"But she's all right."

"She is."

"You don't sound relieved."

"I am relieved, but I'm puzzled." She swirled her coffee in the cup, staring inside as if looking for answers there. "Why did we both have such strong reactions to a couple bottles of wine? Dani knows how to get her drink on. I've never seen her more than a little tipsy, and I haven't gotten sick on booze since my college years, when we'd get an older classmate in our dorm to buy us a bottle of cheap rum and we'd mix it with diet soda."

"Now *I'm* feeling sick." He dusted toast crumbs from his fingertips into his napkin. "I don't know why you're confused. Just because Dani wasn't assaulted, thank God, doesn't mean the two of you weren't drugged."

"For what purpose? I just told you, Mason didn't

molest Dani, and I passed out in the gutter like a common drunk."

"And I rescued you."

"What?" Her eyebrows created a V over her nose. "Rescued me from what?"

"I think I rescued you from Jeffrey." He held out his hand as Sue began to rise from her chair. "Just wait. Did you think he was going to haul you out of the bar in front of witnesses? Did he suggest walking you out or to your car?"

"Yes."

"Maybe he planned to make his move then."

"What move?" Sue hugged herself. "Now you're scaring me."

"I'm not sure, Sue. Those two men, Mason and Jeffrey, or whatever their names are, zeroed in on you and Dani. They slipped you some something and Mason was charged with getting Dani away while Jeffrey was supposed to take care of you."

"'Take care of'? What the hell are you talking about, Mancini?"

"You were kidnapped once and you escaped. What did your captors want with you? Did you think that was going to end just because you escaped?"

This time she did jump up from her chair, and it tipped backward with a thump.

"That was Istanbul. This is DC." She twisted her napkin in front of her.

He raised one eyebrow. "You ever hear of travel by airplane? It's a newfangled invention."

She fired her napkin at him. "Why are you joking? This is serious. You're trying to tell me the people who kidnapped me in Turkey are trying to recapture me here?"

"It's a strong possibility, especially in light of the message Denver sent me."

She stalked to the end of the room, spun around and stalked back. "You said you arrived in DC just yesterday afternoon?"

"Yeah, why?" His heart thumped against his rib cage. He recognized that look on her face—the flared nostrils, the pursed lips, the wide eyes, as if to take in everything in front of them.

"I felt—" she rubbed her upper arms "—like I was being followed the past few weeks. That wasn't you?"

"Nope, but it must've been someone. Your instincts are sharp." He rose from the chair and stationed himself by the window.

"They usually are." She aimed a piercing look at him from her dark eyes and he almost felt the stab in his heart.

He cleared his throat. "Then I think it's clear what we need to do."

"It is? And who's this *we*?"

"Me and you. We need to figure out why you were snatched in the first place and what it has to do with Denver." He rubbed his hands together, the thought of being with Sue, of working beside Sue, making his blood sing.

"I don't think so, Mancini."

"What? Why? Major Denver's life might depend on it, not to mention your safety."

"You and I working together? Spending days and nights together? Heads together?"

"Yeah." He couldn't stop his mouth watering at the prospect, especially when she put it like that.

"We both know that's a prescription for disaster."

"Why is that?" He folded his arms and braced a shoulder against the window, knowing damn well why she thought his idea stunk but wanting to hear it from her lips.

"I… We…" Her cheeks sported two red flags.

He'd never seen Sue flustered before. Could he help it if it gave him a prick of satisfaction?

A knock on the door broke the tension between them, and he silently cursed the hotel staff as Sue crawled back into bed.

The knock repeated, accompanied by a male voice. "Housekeeping. Laundry."

Hunter stepped away from the window, his gait slow. Once Sue got her clothes and got the hell out of here, he'd never see her again. He knew how she operated.

Denver had pegged the wrong man for the job if he wanted intel out of Sue. She wouldn't give him the time of day—even after what they'd shared three years ago.

He swung open the door. "Right on time."

The hotel worker charged into the room with Sue's clothes bagged and draped over his arm. As he brushed past Hunter, the plastic covering the clothing crinkled.

Hunter staggered back. "Whoa."

Before Hunter regained his balance, the clothes slid from the man's arm…revealing a weapon clutched in his hand.

Chapter Three

Sue stared down the barrel of the .38. Her jaw tensed, along with every other muscle in her body.

Hunter made a slight move, and the man with the gun leveled it at her head. "Stay back or I'll take the shot, and it doesn't have to end this way. We just want to talk to her."

"Who's *we*?" Hunter's voice came out in a growl that made the hair on the back of Sue's neck stand on end.

"You need to get lost. You don't want to be involved with her—trust me." The man's lips curled into a lopsided sneer.

Sue's hands tightened into fists around the bed covers. She not only had to stop this guy from shooting her or abducting her; she had to stop him from outing her to Hunter.

With his words, the man had made it clear he didn't have the slightest idea he had a member of Delta Force looming behind him. Good. They'd use that to their advantage. She had to hope the same thought had occurred to Hunter at the same time.

In one movement, Sue yanked the covers over her body and rolled off the bed, toward her would-be kidnapper's knees. She barreled into his legs at about the same time she heard the whiz of his gun's silencer right over her head.

The man grunted and kneed her in the side of the face. Then she felt him go down with a thud, followed by a sickening crack. She yanked the bedspread from her head and came eye to bulging eye with the intruder as Hunter choked off his breath.

The sleeper hold worked like a charm, and the man slumped to the side, his weapon inches from his useless hand.

Panting, Sue scrambled to her feet. "Good work. I thought you'd take advantage of the situation."

"And I'm glad you made that situation possible, even though he could've shot right into those bunched-up covers and hit some part of you." Hunter crouched beside the unconscious man and thumbed up one of his eyelids.

"What now? He's going to come to any minute." And she didn't want this guy talking. Sue dropped to her knees and reached across Hunter, grabbing the gun by the silencer.

The man's lids fluttered and he coughed. His eyes widened and his body bucked.

Sue brought the butt of the gun down on the back of the man's skull and he pitched forward again, a stream of blood spouting from his wound.

Hunter cocked his head. "That's one way to handle it."

"I'm the one he was aiming at. I didn't want to take any chances." She put two fingers against his neck. "I didn't kill him."

"We definitely don't want to leave any dead bodies behind." He pointed at the gun, dangling from her fingers. "You wanna take care of that?"

Rising to her feet, Sue kicked aside the last of the covers wrapped around her ankles and headed for the bathroom. She grabbed a hand towel from the rack and wrapped the gun in its folds.

She returned to the bedroom, placed the gun on the nightstand and knelt across from Hunter, who was rummaging through the man's pockets. "Any luck?"

"A little cash and…this." He held up a cell phone. Then he dropped it and tapped her cheek with his fingertip. "What happened? The side of your face is all red."

"He bashed me in the face on his way down." The throbbing of her cheekbone turned into a tingle under Hunter's gentle touch. "I'll get some ice on it. Phone."

"I'm assuming you have no idea who this guy is or what he wanted?" Hunter's blue eyes narrowed like a jungle cat's.

Had the man's words advising Hunter not to get involved with her registered with Hunter?

She shrugged. "No clue, but I'm guessing he's connected to Jeffrey from last night or maybe the kidnapping in Istanbul or maybe even my suspension from the CIA."

Hunter's head jerked up from the cell phone. "You didn't tell me you'd been suspended. Why?"

"Anonymous tips and emails. Sound familiar?"

"Same tactics used against Major Denver." He scratched his chin with the edge of the phone. "This is getting more and more tangled."

You have no idea, Hunter.

She nudged the inert form on the carpet with her knuckle. "How much time do you think we have?"

"That was a hard blow to the head. I think you bought us fifteen minutes at a minimum." He jabbed his finger at the pile of clothes on the floor. "At least he brought your laundry."

"And look how you tipped him."

He held up one hand. "I just choked him out. You're the one who delivered the lights-out."

Sue ripped the plastic from her slacks and blouse and clutched them to her chest as she backed up toward the bathroom. "I'm going to get dressed, and then we need to leave. I'm not going to explain this situation to hotel security."

"Neither is he." Hunter made a move toward his suitcase parked by the door. "I'll put the Do Not Disturb hanger on the doorknob to buy him some time. When he comes to, he'll want to hightail it out of here."

"You're right." She tapped her cheek. "Can you grab some ice from the machine for my face while I'm getting dressed?"

"I'm on it."

As she stepped into her slacks, she heard the door

open and close, and she eased out a sigh. Who the hell was that in the other room? Was The Falcon right? Had she been made?

She wouldn't put those strong-arm tactics past the Agency, either, so it could be someone following up on her suspension. Her life was becoming more complex than usual—and the appearance of Hunter Mancini had just added to the mayhem. But what sweet mayhem.

Those blue eyes of his held the same hypnotic quality she hadn't been able to resist in Paris—even though hooking up with Hunter had broken all the rules. She hadn't given a damn then, and she didn't give a damn right now.

She needed someone on her side. Someone she could trust. Someone she could reach out and grab—unlike The Falcon, a nameless, faceless contact spitting orders at her.

The banging of the door made her jump. She smoothed the blouse over her hips and straightened her spine. Time to get to work.

She exited the bathroom and almost ran into Hunter, dangling a bag of ice from his fingertips.

"You looking for another black eye?"

"I don't think I'm going to get a black eye, but I can see a bruise forming on my cheek." She took the bag from him and pressed it against her face with a shiver. "You have toiletries in the bathroom."

"Thanks, I'll grab them, and then we'll get out of here."

"Did you check his phone?"

"Password protected." He patted the pocket of his button-up shirt. "We'll figure it out."

Sue stepped over their conked-out guest on the floor on the way to her boots. Perching on the edge of the bed, she pulled them on. "You have everything? Do you need to check out?"

Hunter stuffed his toiletry bag into his suitcase, along with the wrapped-up gun, and zipped it. "I'll call the hotel later and tell them I had a change of plans. I don't want housekeeping coming up here anytime soon, not until our friend wakes up and gets out of Dodge."

"Do you have another place in mind?" She strode to the credenza and grabbed her purse, her own weapon stashed in the side pocket.

"Your place?"

Her head whipped around and she swallowed hard. "No."

"From the outside, the place looks big enough for the two of us." He drew a cross over his heart. "I promise not to undress you and put you to bed anymore—unless you need it."

She snorted. "I'm not going to need it, and staying at my place would be a bad, bad idea. You don't think these goons...whoever they are...know where I live?"

"Your building looks secure and we're both armed." He tipped his head at the man on the floor. "I think we can handle anything that comes our way."

Hunter wouldn't be able to handle anything in that townhouse.

"I think it would be best if you found yourself another hotel." She hitched her purse over her shoulder. "I may even join you."

Hunter's blue eyes darkened. "Does this mean you're gonna work with me to figure out if the guys who snatched you are the ones working against Denver? 'Cause you were dead-set against that before this guy came along and pulled a gun on you."

"Exactly. He made me change my mind."

"Maybe I should thank him—or at least make him more comfortable." Hunter returned to the bathroom and came out swinging a hand towel.

He crouched beside the man and wrapped the cloth around his head, pressing it against his wound. Then he jerked back.

"We need to leave—now."

"Is he coming around?" Sue lunged for the hotel door and plucked the hanger from the handle.

"His color is coming back. It shouldn't be too much longer now." He stepped back from the body on the floor and grasped the handle of his suitcase. "Lead the way."

Sue held the door open for him as he wheeled his suitcase into the hallway. She eased the door closed and slipped the Do Not Disturb sign onto the handle.

When they got to the elevator, Hunter punched the button for a floor on the parking level.

"You have a car?"

"A rental. Do you have any suggestions for my next stop?"

"Is money a consideration, or no?" Her gaze flicked over his expensive suitcase, black leather jacket and faded jeans, which told her nothing except the man was still hotter than blazes.

"No." He lifted one eyebrow toward the black hair swept back from his forehead.

"Then I'd suggest the Hay-Adams. It's in the heart of everything, too crowded for us to stand out, too busy for us to be accosted at gunpoint in the parking lot, too expensive not to have security cameras everywhere."

"That's where your friend, Dani, was taken last night."

"Exactly. Maybe we can do a little research on those two guys from last night." She patted her purse. "I didn't tell you I took a picture of Jeffrey."

"A selfie of the two of you?"

Her brows snapped together. "Insurance in case he raped and murdered me."

"Quick thinking. I didn't get a good look at either one of them when I snuck into the bar last night for surveillance."

"Not very good surveillance, then." She clicked her tongue.

"I didn't want to out myself by staring."

The elevator dinged, and Hunter jabbed at the button to hold open the doors. "After you."

Once he loaded his bag into his rental car and pulled out of the parking structure, she directed him to the next hotel. He maneuvered through the busy streets like a pro, and they left the car with the valet in front of the hotel.

She hovered at his elbow as he checked in, drumming her fingers on the reception desk. She'd played up her fear over returning to her own place, as there was no way in hell she could have him inside her townhouse, but she'd have to explain somehow that she felt perfectly safe returning home on her own. She couldn't stay in this hotel with Hunter—not again.

She had very little self-control when it came to this man—and she needed her self-control.

"Thank you, Mr. and Mrs. Roberts. Let us know if you need anything." The clerk smiled as she shoved a key card toward Sue.

Sue blinked and then swept the card from the counter and pocketed it.

As Hunter wheeled his suitcase toward the elevator, she hissed into his ear, "Who the hell is Mr. Roberts? Or Mrs. Roberts, for that matter?"

"That would be us, dear." He winked at her. "You're not the only one who knows how to play spy. I have a whole new identity for my stay in DC. I told you that I'm not here on official duty and I don't want my actions to be tracked."

"You have all the credentials?" She tilted her head. "Driver's license, credit cards?"

"I do. Mr. Roberts even has a passport."

She held the elevator door open for him as he dragged his suitcase inside. "I feel so humbled now that I know how easy it is for anyone to fake a new ID."

"Spare me." He nudged her shoulder. "As if you don't know all about that. Half the time the Agency can't locate someone, it's because he or she adopted a new identity."

"Just like I'm sure Jeffrey on my phone is not really a Jeffrey."

"He must've followed us back to my hotel and notified the second shift…if he was in on it."

"I'm pretty sure that was no coincidence—passing out and then the attempted abduction this morning. They didn't expect you to be there, that's for sure."

The elevator settled on their floor, and they exited. Sue got her card out when they reached the room and slid it home. She poked her head inside before widening the door for Hunter and his bag. "Just making sure nobody is here before us."

"They were good last night, but not that good." He wheeled his suitcase into the corner and then bounced on the edge of the king-size bed. "Plenty of room for the two of us—your side and my side."

No time to burst his bubble now. She curled her lips into a perfunctory smile. "Should we get to work on the phone now before it's deactivated?"

"Do you have any tricks of the trade to find out or bypass the password?" He fished the would-be kidnapper's phone from his pocket and tossed it onto the bed beside him.

"I might have a few tricks up my sleeve." She wedged a knee on the bed and scooped up the phone. "In the meantime, why don't you have a look at Jeffrey's picture just in case? We could send it in for facial recognition—if I were still in good standing with the CIA."

"Yeah, I was counting on you having all the Agency's resources at your disposal. Now I'll just have to do this the sneaky way."

She paused as she drew her phone from her purse, holding it in midair. "Are you telling me you have a contact in the CIA? Someone to do your bidding?"

"Do my bidding? I wouldn't put it like that, but yeah, I have a little helper."

Shaking her head, she said, "That agency has more leaks than a colander."

She tapped her photos to bring up Jeffrey's picture. "Give me your number and I'll send it to you."

"I can just look at it on your phone." He snapped his fingers.

"It's better if we have a copy, anyway." She held her finger poised above her display. "Number?"

"Is this your sneaky way of getting my cell? You could just ask, you know." He rattled off his cell number and she entered it into her phone.

Actually, it was just her sneaky way of keeping him away from her phone. She didn't keep pictures on her cell, but she didn't need Hunter looking at her text messages.

She tapped her screen with a flourish. "There. The picture is on its way. Now, I'll get to work on this phone."

She dragged a chair to the window and kicked up her feet onto the chair across from it. She powered on the stranger's cell, which they'd turned off to avoid any tracking, but turning it back on couldn't be helped.

"This guy your type?" Hunter held up his phone with Jeffrey's mug on the display.

"Tall, dark and handsome?" She snorted. "You could say that."

Hunter brought the phone up to his nose and squinted. "How tall was he?"

"Tall enough." Sue eyed Hunter's lanky frame stretched out on the bed, his feet hanging off the edge.

With a smile curling her lip, she hunched over the cell phone again.

Sue clicked through the phone to access a few of the backdoor methods she'd learned at the Agency for bypassing a password to get into a phone. These worked especially well for burner phones like this one—and she knew a thing or two about burner phones.

She glanced up as Hunter swung his legs off the side of the bed, hunching over his phone, his back to her. Seconds later, his cell buzzed and he murmured a few words into his phone.

He must've reached his secret CIA contact—one who hadn't been suspended from the Agency. She just hoped he knew to keep her name off his lips.

A few taps later, the gunman's phone came to life in her hand. She slid another glance toward Hunter's back and launched the man's text messages and recent contacts.

Hunter ended his own call and stood up, stretching his arms to the ceiling. "I'm going to grab a soda from the machine down the hall. Want something?"

"Something diet, please." Tucking her hair behind one ear, she glanced up and pasted a smile on her lips.

When the door closed behind Hunter, Sue began transferring the data from the stranger's phone to her own—contacts, pictures, texts and call history.

When she reached the last bit of data, Hunter charged into the room, a can of soda in each hand. "Any luck with that?"

She slumped in her chair, clutching the phone in her hand. "Not yet."

Then she tapped the display one last time to erase everything the man had on his burner phone.

Chapter Four

Hunter snapped open Sue's can of soda and leaned over her shoulder, placing it on the table in front of her. The click of the aluminum against the wood made her jump and flush to the roots of her dark hair as she jerked her head around.

"Did I scare you?" He dropped his hand to her shoulder briefly.

"I didn't realize you were right behind me."

"You were too engrossed in that phone." He opened his own soda and sank to the edge of the bed. "It's a bummer you can't get anything from it."

She placed the phone facedown on the table and spun it around. "None of my tricks are working. Phones are getting more and more sophisticated now and harder to break into. I think the CIA needs to get its cyber division on this to come up with some methods to bypass the new security measures."

"Speaking of the Agency and security measures, my contact thinks he can run Jeffrey's picture through face recognition. If he's on the intelligence radar, we should get a hit."

"He?" Sue twisted the tab off her can. "Is he stationed here in DC?"

"Oh no, you don't. I don't give up my sources, not even to other sources." He leveled a finger at her. "And that should give you some sense of comfort."

She tucked one long leg beneath her. "Did you ever tell anyone about us? I mean our brief affair in Paris?"

Brief? Had their affair been brief? He'd been so lost in Sue, lost in Paris that the world had seemed light-years away, and he'd felt suspended in time. Ever since then, he'd measured everything in terms of before Sue and after Sue. And everything before seemed to be a pale imitation of what came after.

Under her penetrating dark eyes, he felt a flush creep up from his chest. "I did tell a few people—my Delta Force team. That's all. It's how Major Denver knew to task me with contacting you."

"I see." She braced one elbow on the table and buried her chin in her palm.

"Did you?" He held his breath for some reason.

"No."

The word didn't come out as forceful as the expression on her face. She *had* told someone.

"Our affair was a mistake." She sat back in her chair and crossed her arms over her chest.

Hunter gulped down his soda until it fizzed in his nose and tears came to his eyes. So much for getting Sue into bed tonight.

He wiped the back of his hand across his tingling nose. "Two people, even someone from Delta Force and someone from the CIA, enjoying some R and R in Paris, off duty. As far as I remember, our pillow talk didn't include any state or military secrets. Why is that a mistake?"

She drew her bottom lip between her teeth and hunched her shoulders.

"Oh." He crushed his can with one hand. "You weren't off duty, were you?"

Her eyes narrowed. "You need a haircut."

"What?" He skimmed the palm of his hand over the top of his short hair. "Where did that come from?"

"I know just the place." She sat up ramrod straight and snatched her cell phone from the desk. She tapped her screen and nodded. "It's called T.J.'s Barbershop, and it's downtown."

"Does this have something to do with what happened this morning?"

Sue stood up, tilting her head to the side. "Do you trust me, Hunter?"

Did he? She'd indulged in a fling with him while she was on an assignment in Paris, without telling him, and then left him high and dry in their love nest without a backward glance and disappeared. He never heard from her again. She wouldn't take him back to her place here in DC. And she'd just been suspended from the Agency.

Her dark lashes fluttered as the sun from the window set fire to the mahogany highlights in her hair. Her lips parted, waiting for his answer.

"Yeah, I trust you, Sue."

"Good." She reached across the table and tugged her jacket from the back of the chair. "Haircut at T.J.'s. They take walk-ins and you're going to ask for Walid."

HUNTER DRUMMED HIS thumbs against the steering wheel as he waited for Sue outside her townhouse in Georgetown. She neglected to invite him in, claiming she'd be just a few minutes.

A few minutes later, true to her word, she appeared on her porch, wheeling one bag behind her, another slung over her shoulder. She waved to someone coming up the steps, clutching a small child by the hand, exchanged a few words with this person and then jogged across the street to his rental car.

He popped the trunk and hopped out of the car.

"Bad idea to leave the car. Parking enforcement love giving tickets on this block." She nudged up the trunk.

"I haven't gone anywhere." He collapsed the suitcase handle and hoisted the bag into the car. "This, too?"

"Got it." She swung her shoulder bag into the trunk on top of her suitcase.

When they got back into the car, he glanced at her as he started the engine. "I suppose you're coming inside with me for the haircut I don't need."

"Of course."

"Are you going to tell me what this is about?"

"I'm pretty sure this barbershop is connected to the group I've been tracking, the same one Denver was looking into before he went AWOL, if his intel is correct."

Hunter's pulse ticked up a few notches. Progress. "You're *pretty* sure, not positive?"

"I got a tip about T.J.'s, but apparently it couldn't be verified."

"And now I'm going to try to verify again. Walid?" He made the turn she indicated onto an even busier street than the one they'd left.

"He's the key." She tapped on the window as they crawled through traffic. "You're going to make a right in a few miles at Sixteenth Street. There won't be any parking on the street at this time of the day, so we'll leave the car in a public lot."

"Are we doing anything in the barbershop, whether or not Walid is there?"

"I am." She dug through her purse and cupped a small black device in her palm.

Hunter raised his brows. "A camera? A bug?"

"Both video and sound. I'm leaving it there, regardless of what happens."

"Do you need me to do anything?"

"A little distraction wouldn't hurt, but don't go overboard and make them suspicious." She poked his thigh with her knuckle. "I know you D-boys like to come in with guns blazing, but this is a little subtler than that."

He raised two fingers. "I'm the height of discretion. I didn't even chase after you after you dumped me in Paris."

"I didn't dump you, Hunter." She folded her hands

in her lap. "The affair had run its course. I had some-where else I needed to be."

"There's nowhere else I wanted to be." He squinted at the brake lights of the car in front of him.

She turned her head to look out the window, her dark hair creating a silky veil over her face. "It was… nice."

Nice? Not exactly the word he'd use for the pas-sion they'd shared, but he'd take it for now.

Rapping on the window, she said, "Next right."

He maneuvered the car around the corner into a bustling business district missing the genteel leafi-ness of Georgetown but making up for it in sheer energy.

"Is that it?" He pointed to a revolving barbershop pole on the next corner.

"Yeah. Look for a lot."

Almost two blocks away, Hunter pulled the car in to a public parking lot and paid the attendant. As he and Sue trooped up the sidewalk back toward the barbershop, he shoved his hands into the pockets of his jacket, against the chill in the air. Spring had sprung, but nobody had told the DC weatherman yet.

Sue's low-heeled boots clicked beside him. She'd done a quick change of clothes at her place, replac-ing her black slacks with a pair of black jeans that hugged her in all the right places. Every place on Sue's body was the right place, as far as he was con-cerned.

When they reached T.J.'s, Hunter swung open the

door, causing a little bell to jingle wildly. Three barbers turned their heads toward the new customers.

The one on the end paused, clippers in the air. "Can I help you? Cut?"

"Just a cleanup." Hunter ran a hand over his head, the short ends tickling the palm of his hand. "Edge the neck."

"Sure, have a seat."

As he perched on the edge of a worn love seat, Sue remained standing, facing a rack of magazines, her hand clenched lightly at her side.

Hunter cleared his throat. "Is Walid around? My friend recommended Walid."

Did two of the barbers stop clipping at the same time?

"Walid?" The man on the end who'd welcomed him shook his head. "He doesn't work here anymore. Hasn't been here for a while."

"No problem. Thought I'd check."

"I hope this doesn't take too long, James." Sue grabbed a sports magazine and leafed through it.

"You're the one who wanted me to get the cut, honey. We can leave right now if you want."

The barber in the middle chuckled as he handed a mirror to his customer. "I'm ready for you. Shouldn't take long. Step over to the sink."

The last thing he wanted was some dude washing his hair. He held up his hands and took a step back—right into Sue.

She drilled a knuckle into the center of his spine.

"Go ahead, James. I saw a drugstore down the block and I have a few things to pick up. Take your time."

"You're not in a hurry anymore?" He shuffled toward the barber holding out a white towel.

"You might as well get the full treatment." She tapped him with the rolled-up magazine in her hand, and it slipped out of her hand and fell to the floor at the feet of the barber at the first station.

Hunter followed his guy toward the row of sinks, leaving the magazine on the floor.

The first barber set down the hairdryer he'd just picked up and bent over to retrieve the magazine.

Sue reached out, wedging one hand against the magazine rack as she reached with the other. "Oh, thank you."

Hunter figured she'd just placed her device and got confirmation a minute later when she called from the door. "Meet me at the coffeehouse next to the drugstore when you're done."

He lifted his hand before he went under the warm spray.

Thirty minutes later, he managed to get out of T.J.'s with a little off the sides and a cleaned-up neckline. He loped down the street and ducked into the coffeehouse.

Sue looked up from her phone and wiggled her fingers.

He ordered a coffee on the way, when what he really wanted was lunch, and pulled out the chair across from her. "I'm guessing you did what you went to T.J.'s to do."

"Nice cut." She peered at him over the top of her cell phone and then turned it around to face him, showing him a video of the barbershop in real time. "But then I already knew that."

"What did you make of Walid's absence? Do you believe them?"

"I'm not sure, but the fact that they knew Walid was a plus. I know that's the barbershop that featured in my intel." She tapped her phone on the tabletop. "And now I'll have an eye on what goes on there."

"Is that why you dropped by your place—to pick up spy gadgets?"

"That and to change clothes and pack a bag. I meant it when I said I was going to stay with you at the hotel."

"Déjà vu all over again."

She opened her mouth, probably to correct him, but the barista saved him by calling his name.

"My coffee." He pushed back from the table and picked up his drink.

When he returned, she was hunched over her phone again. "Any activity?"

"Plenty, but not the kind I'm interested in." She swirled her cup and took a sip.

"What about the other phone?"

"The other phone?" Her paper cup slipped from her hand and rolled on the table.

He picked it up and shook it. "Lucky it's empty. The phone I took off the intruder."

"I turned that off for now. I'm afraid it can be tracked or pinged." She folded a napkin into a small square. "I wasn't having any luck with the password, anyway."

"We still have his fingerprints on that gun. I'm hoping to get some help with that."

"Yeah, that gun." She dropped her phone into her purse. "Sounds like you have more contacts at the Agency than I do. Maybe your contacts can get me my job back."

"You weren't fired."

"Not yet." She twisted up her mouth on one side. "Now I know how Denver feels."

"You think you're being set up?"

"I don't know what to think." She stuffed her napkin inside her cup. "Are you ready?"

He drained his lukewarm coffee from his cup and stood. "Let's go."

He guided Sue through traffic on the sidewalk, as her phone engrossed her and she barely looked up.

When they got to the car, he opened the passenger's door for her. "I hope you don't walk around the city with your nose in your phone like that all the time."

She held up her cell as she slid onto the seat. "Just when I'm watching surveillance video."

"Do you know what you're watching for?"

"Not really. I'll know it when I see it."

"And then you'll let me know, right?" He caught the door before slamming it. "Right?"

Sue answered without looking up. "Of course."

Hunter scuffed back around to the driver's side. Why did he feel like he just got used in that barbershop? He didn't even need a haircut.

As he got behind the wheel, his phone buzzed. He checked the display. "Perfect timing. My contact has some info on Jeffrey."

"Did he send it through?" Sue finally glanced up from her phone, her eyes shining.

"No. He doesn't want to expose the information by emailing or texting it. He's going to leave it for me in a mailbox."

A laugh bubbled from her lips. "You're joking."

"Why would I be joking? He sent me the address of a vacant house in Fredericksburg, Virginia, and he's leaving the information in the mailbox." He tapped his phone to bring up his GPS and then tossed it to Sue. "Can you enter the address for me?"

"Fredericksburg? That's at least an hour away." She held his phone in front of her face.

"You don't expect him to leave it outside the gates of Langley, do you?"

"No." She turned down the news on the radio. "I take it back. It's an ingenious method of communication. I'll have to remember that ploy for my next covert operation."

"This *is* your next covert operation." He gave her the address of the house and then headed out of town, following the GPS directions south.

The landscape rolled out the green carpet as they hit the highway to Virginia. The recent rains had created a verdant emerald border along either side of the highway that rushed by in a blur.

"Pretty, isn't it?" Sue had slumped in her seat, resting the side of her head against the window.

"I was just thinking that, myself." Hunter glanced at his rearview mirror and furrowed his brow. "That truck's coming up fast on my tail."

"We have two lanes. He can go around." Hunching forward, Sue peered into the side mirror. "Idiot."

"He must've heard you."

Hunter tracked the truck as it veered into the left lane and started gaining on them. He eased off the gas to give the behemoth plenty of room to pass and move over.

As the truck drew abreast of his car, it slowed down.

"Jerk. What does he want? I'm not getting into a road rage situation with him."

Gripping the steering wheel, Hunter glanced to his left and swore. "He has a gun!"

Chapter Five

Sue threw out a hand and wedged it against the dashboard as Hunter slammed on the brakes and the car fishtailed on the road. Her gaze flew to the side mirror and an oncoming car blowing its horn and swerving toward the shoulder.

She hunched her shoulders and braced for the impact. Instead, the car lurched forward as Hunter punched the gas pedal. Her head snapped forward and back, hitting the headrest.

The truck to their left had slowed down when they had, and as the little rental leaped ahead eating the asphalt beneath it, the truck roared back to life.

Hunter shouted, "My gun! Get my gun under the seat."

Sue bent forward, her hand scrabbling beneath the driver's seat between Hunter's legs. Her fingers curled around the cold metal and she yanked it free.

When she popped up, she screamed as Hunter zoomed toward the car in front of them.

He pumped the brake pedal, and their tires squealed in protest. The truck had pulled up next to the car in front of them, veering to the right, almost clipping the left bumper and then jerking back, probably realizing he had the wrong target.

"He's gonna hang back and wait for us again." Hunter's gun nestled in her hand and she slipped her finger onto the trigger.

"You know what to do." Hunter held his body stiffly, pressing it against his seat back.

Sue released her seat belt with a click and leaned into the driver's seat, practically resting her chest against Hunter's.

As the truck drew level with them, she thrust the barrel of Hunter's gun out the open window.

She caught a glimpse of the face in the window, eyes and mouth wide open, before the driver of the truck suddenly dropped back, tires screeching.

The car behind the truck honked long and hard, and Sue retreated to her seat, the gun still clutched in her hand, finger on the trigger. "Someone's gonna call 911 and report this, report our license plates."

"Then it's a good thing that sap Roberts is renting this car and not me."

"Unless the cops respond to the scene and pull you over."

"Not. Gonna. Happen." Hunter cut in front of the car ahead of them and accelerated onto the off-ramp, checking his rearview mirror.

"Is the truck following us?"

"If he can see what we're doing, he will."

They curved to the left, and Hunter blew through the stop sign at the T in the road, making the turn.

He pointed at the windshield. "Shopping mall ahead. We're going into that parking structure."

Sue twisted her head over her left shoulder, scanning the road and the off-ramp behind them.

"Is he coming?"

"I can't see around the bend in the road. It's no longer a straight shot."

"Good." Hunter wheeled into the structure and climbed a few levels. He parked between two SUVs, pulling the car all the way in to the parking slot.

He left the engine idling and closed his eyes, drawing in a deep breath. "Should we stay here or go inside?"

"I don't like the idea of being a sitting duck." Her gaze darted to the side mirror for the hundredth time since they'd parked, and they'd been here just about thirty seconds.

"If we head into the mall and they locate the car, they can stake it out. Wait for us."

"We don't know what kind of firepower they have." She licked her dry lips. "They could come up behind us and blast the car. We can't hold them off with one gun."

"Where's yours?"

"It's in my bag in the trunk."

"Bad place for it, Chandler."

She smacked her hand against the dashboard. "I have an idea. I have another camera in my bag of tricks. I can stick it on the back window of the car. That way, we can see if anyone approaches the car while we're inside. If not, and we give it enough time, we'll make our escape."

"I can live with that." He peeled her fingers from his gun still in her grip and wedged by the side of her hip. "I'm packing this and you'd better take yours. We still need to get to Fredericksburg and that mailbox."

She flicked the door handle and Hunter raised his hand. "Hang on. Let me check the area first."

When he finished his surveillance, he tapped on her window. "All clear...for now."

She got out of the car and immediately grabbed Hunter's forearm as her knees gave out.

Curling an arm around her, he asked, "Are you all right?"

"Didn't realize that wild ride had shaken me up so much." She stomped her feet on the ground. "Just need to get my bearings."

"Take all the time you need." His fingers pressed the side of her hip through her jeans.

"Thanks, and thanks for getting us out of that mess...whatever that mess was."

"I'm not convinced they were going to shoot us."

"Really?" She shifted away from him and tilted her head. "He had a gun."

"So did the guy in the hotel room. He could've shot both of us the minute he walked in with the laundry—had a silencer and everything. He didn't." Hunter tugged on his earlobe. "What do you think they want? An interrogation?"

Sue lifted her shoulders up and down in a quick

movement. "I'm not sure, but let's not stand around here any longer than we have to."

He popped the trunk for her and stood guard as she rummaged inside her duffel bag and pulled out her weapon and a small plastic bag containing the same type of camera she'd stuck in the barbershop. Was that where they'd been picked up? Had asking about Walid marked them as hostile intruders?

When she finished, Hunter slammed the trunk closed and said, "I know what I want to do in that mall while we're killing time."

"See a movie?"

"Not a bad idea as long as we get hot dogs and popcorn. I'm starving." He patted his flat stomach. "Evasive driving always works up my appetite."

"I'm glad someone can eat. I feel like I'm gonna throw up." Sue zipped her gun into the side pocket of her purse and strapped the purse across her body.

They took the elevator to the third floor and a pedestrian bridge that crossed to the mall.

The normalcy of people shopping, having coffee and eating made Sue blink. The world still revolved and people still lived their lives while others, like her and Hunter, had to protect them from the harsh truths. She'd been aware of those truths for far too long, thanks to her father.

Hunter tipped back his head and sniffed. "Ahh, mall food—cinnamon, grease, cookies and pizza— what more could you ask?"

"Some real food." She tugged on his sleeve.

"There are a couple of restaurants upstairs. We need some privacy."

They rode up the escalator together, which gave her a better view of the indoor mall—and the people in it. Hunter couldn't fool her. Beneath his joking manner—and hers—the tension simmered like a live wire.

She dragged him into a chain restaurant with a five-page plastic menu, and they both ordered ice tea after they sat down.

Sue sucked down some tea, and when she came up for air, she asked, "Do you think they were trying to run us off the road by shooting out our window or tire?"

"Or they were trying to warn you. Maybe someone saw us at the barbershop or the guys at the barbershop placed a call and set someone on us. Where'd you get the barbershop tip?"

She ran a finger across the seam of her lips. "That's top secret stuff. You have your sources and I have mine."

"Yeah, but my source is one of your fellow agents. Who's your source?" Hunter picked up a couple of menus and tapped them on the table before sliding one across to her.

"Can't tell you that." If she started down that road with Hunter, there's no telling where it might end—probably with Drake.

"Then only you know if the intel about the barbershop is legit—seems that it was, if five minutes after my haircut we're being chased down the highway."

Why would The Falcon tell her the barbershop hadn't panned out? Had someone there recognized her, realizing she probably knew all about the barbershop, anyway?

Hunter pinged her menu and she glanced up.

"Are you feeling better? You're going to order something?"

She ran her fingertip down the page of items. "Probably just some soup."

When the waitress came over, Sue ordered some cream of broccoli soup and Hunter went all out with a burger and fries.

"You haven't checked the barbershop." He prodded her phone with his knuckle. "Maybe we'll see someone making a call or coming inside."

"And let's not forget your rental car." She picked up her phone and tapped the display to toggle between the two camera views. "I'm not going back to that parking lot if there's any suspicious activity going on."

She turned the time back on the barbershop video and hunched forward on the table to share the view with Hunter. "There's you getting your haircut."

"Don't remind me." He huffed out a breath. "You can skip that part because, I can tell you, one other guy came in after me and spent the entire time complaining about his prostate."

"Sounds fascinating." She flicked her fingers at the images. "Did you give him a good tip? Maybe that's why they were chasing us in that truck."

"That's a good sign."

"What?" She stopped the video.

"You can sort of laugh about it after you nearly collapsed getting out of the car."

She smacked the back of his hand. "I didn't almost collapse. My knees were a little wobbly. That's all."

"That's right. You're the badass agent who escaped from a gaggle of terrorists in Istanbul. You never told me about that whole incident, and that's what I should've been asking you about all this time because that's really the connection to Denver."

"Well, we did get sidetracked." And with any luck she'd sidetrack him again. Her so-called abduction was the last thing she wanted to discuss with Hunter…second to the last thing.

Sue clapped her hands together. "Our food's here."

"I thought you weren't hungry." Hunter thanked the waitress and asked for ketchup.

"I recovered." She dipped her spoon into the soup and blew on the liquid.

As they ate lunch, they kept checking back and forth between the two videos on her phone and nobody went near Hunter's rental in the parking lot.

"I guess we lost them." Sue broke up a cracker between her fingers. "I just wish I knew who they were and what they wanted."

"Maybe they just wanted to warn you away from the barbershop."

"How'd they know we were there?"

"They could have their own surveillance devices there if it's a hotbed meeting place for terrorists.

They made you when you went into the shop, and someone came out to track you...warn you."

"That's some warning—a gun out the car window."

"No shots fired when they could've easily taken one at the window." He dragged a fry through the puddle of ketchup on his plate. "Same with the guy in the hotel room this morning. They don't seem very eager to kill you. They want something else from you."

"I can't imagine what." She picked up her phone and studied the display. "I'm okay with heading back to the car now. We want to get to that mailbox before someone beats us to it."

On the ride to Fredericksburg, Sue sat forward in her seat, her spine stiff, her gaze darting between the side-view mirror and out the window.

"I think we're in the clear." Hunter adjusted the rearview mirror, anyway. "However they got onto us, it wasn't through GPS or we'd have a tail right now."

"If it's GPS, they can afford to keep their distance and ambush us at the mailbox." Her fingers curled around the edge of the seat. "Do you think they put something on your car?"

"When could they have done that? They wouldn't have been able to identify this car at the hotel."

"Unless Jeffrey watched you pick me up from the gutter and load me into your car."

"Didn't happen, and even if they did ID you in the barbershop, which seems likely, they couldn't have known which car was mine or where we parked before we got there."

"So, you think they caught me on surveillance at the barbershop and followed us to our car from there and then tailed us and made their move on the highway?"

"That seems the most probable to me. What they wanted?" He scratched his chin. "I still don't have a clue, but then you haven't been completely open with me, have you?"

Sue's stomach flip-flopped. "What do you mean?"

"Why that barbershop? What do you know about it? Who's there? What are they doing there? Who gave you the tip?"

She released a slow breath through parted lips. "I just can't tell you some of that, Hunter, and some I don't know. Can you be patient?"

"I've waited this long."

He mumbled the words under his breath and she gave him a sharp glance. Did he mean he'd waited long enough for the information or for her?

She felt like she'd been waiting for him, too, but she'd had her orders.

She pinched the bridge of her tingling nose. Hunter was here under an assumed name on unofficial duty. The Falcon didn't have to know, did he?

"Are you okay?" Hunter brushed a hand against her thigh.

Sue blinked. "I'm good. We're almost there."

Hunter followed the voice on his phone's GPS to a leafy neighborhood in an upscale suburb. He spot-

ted the house for sale on the left and drove to the end
of the block to make a U-turn.

As he rolled to a stop at the curb, he said, "Sit
tight. I'll run around and get it."

"You're driving. I'll hop out and grab it."

"I don't want you to." He put a hand on her shoulder.

Goosebumps raced down her arms. "You just got
through assuring me we weren't followed from the
mall."

"I don't think we were, but why expose yourself?"
He grabbed the handle and popped the door. "This
is my contact, my setup."

"Knock yourself out, Mancini." She slumped
down in her seat just in case his concerns came to
fruition.

He bolted from the car and strode to the curb. He
flipped open the mailbox and reached inside. Wav-
ing a cardboard tube in the air, he hustled back to
the car and tossed the package into her lap. "Got it."

As Hunter peeled away from the curb and punched
the accelerator, Sue stuck her eye to one hole in the
tube. "There's stuff rolled up in here."

"Can you get it out?"

"Hang on." She licked the tips of two fingers and
stuck them inside the cardboard roll. She pressed her
fingers against the paper inside the tube and dragged
them toward the opening. "I think I have them."

When the rolled-up papers peeked over the edge
of the tube, she pinched them between her thumb
and forefinger and worked them out.

She unrolled the slick photograph paper first and flattened the pictures on her lap. "It's Jeffrey."

The first photo showed the man who'd chatted her up at the bar last night in conversation with another man, whom she recognized.

She held up the picture to Hunter. "Here's Jeffrey meeting with a known terrorist, proving you were right about him and his motives."

She flipped through a few more pictures in that sequence and turned over another batch. She gasped as her gaze locked onto Jeffrey's companion in the next picture.

"What is it? Who's that?" Hunter pumped the brakes to slow the car.

She knew the identity of the man in the picture with Jeffrey, all right.

But if she told Hunter how she really knew this man, she'd reveal the truth about her real function with the CIA—that she was a double agent, had been one for years and wouldn't be able to help him clear Denver without blowing her own cover.

So, she did what she'd been doing with Hunter ever since the day she met him in Paris—she lied.

Chapter Six

Hunter's gut twisted as he glanced at Sue's face. This had to be bad. Denver?

He careened to the side of the road and skidded to a stop on the soft shoulder. "Show me."

Pinching the photo between her thumb and forefinger, she turned it around to face him. "H-he's a known terrorist."

Hunter squinted at the picture of Jeffrey talking to a man in the shadow of a building, a hoodie covering his head and half his face.

"You recognize him?" He flicked his finger at the photo, hitting it and causing it to sway back and forth. "How can you tell who he is?"

"I just know. I've seen him before…in other surveillance photos." She stacked the picture on top of the others in her lap.

"What does my guy say about these pictures? Any commentary or am I supposed to know what this all means?"

Sue stuck the tube to her eye. "There's a piece of paper in here."

Hunter threw the car into Park as Sue fished the paper from the tube.

She shook it out and started reading aloud. "Face recognition matched with these pictures in our database. The guy with the dark jacket is Amir Dawud, who's gone underground since the bombing in Brussels. We don't know the guy in the...hoodie, but if he's with Jeffrey, he's probably involved in terror activity."

"The entire CIA doesn't know that guy and doesn't have a file on him, but you recognized him from a half-profile shot?"

Sue shuffled through the pictures in her lap and held the photo in front of her again, her head to one side. "Well, I thought it was someone we had ID'd from a previous campaign, but I could be wrong."

"Regardless—" he put the car in drive and rolled away from the side of the road "—Jeffrey is definitely connected to a terrorist organization and his meeting with you last night was no coincidence."

"I'm just glad nothing happened to Dani." Sue busied herself rolling up the pictures and paper again and stuffing them inside the tube.

"I wanna get ahold of one of these guys who keeps threatening you and ask him what he wants." Hunter clenched the steering wheel with both hands. "Did they ever get around to interrogating you when they kidnapped you?"

"No." Sue closed her eyes and sighed. "I guess my connection to Major Denver is tenuous unless we find out what they want from me—and I'm not going to give them that chance."

"This could all be related to your suspension. Do you think someone's trying to set you up at work to discredit any information you might have about Denver?"

"But I don't have any information about Denver." She tapped on the window. "Are we going back to the hotel now?"

"I was, unless you have somewhere else you need to be." He nodded toward her purse on the floor. "You should check the barbershop camera for any developments. Since we left there, we were shot at and almost run off the road."

Sue hesitated before bending forward and plunging her hand into her purse.

He quirked an eyebrow in her direction. "Are you okay?"

Clasping the phone to her chest, she slumped in her seat. "Just tired."

"Do you want me to look?" He held out his hand.

"You're driving. Keep your eyes on the road." She scooted up in her seat and tapped her display several times. "I'll review the footage from earlier—about the time we lost the car following us and turned in to that mall."

Hunter glanced in his rearview mirror. "Nobody tailing us now."

"That's good. It means someone picked us up at the barbershop as opposed to putting a tracker on your car, or something like that." She raised the phone in the air and tilted it back and forth. "They're cutting hair. That's all I see."

"What did you expect to see? What's supposed to be going on at the shop?"

"I'm not sure it's a *what* so much as a *who*."

"And you don't see the *who* there?"

"No."

"And you'd know him if you saw him because you never forget a terrorist's face. You're good."

"I've been at this awhile, Hunter. I've studied pictures, video, been involved in interrogations."

"That's why I think you can help clear Denver's name." He flexed his fingers on the steering wheel. "If we can match up his contacts with your knowledge of these groups and their personnel, I think we might get a few hits. He seems to think so. That's why he sent me out here to connect with you."

Not that anyone had to twist his arm. He'd wanted to contact Sue so many times over the past few years, but she'd left him and he was done chasing after women who didn't want him.

Sue studied her phone for a few more minutes and then slipped it back into her purse. "Nothing but haircuts."

They drove the remaining miles to the hotel in a silence heavy enough to fog the windows of the car.

Hunter shifted a glance to the side at Sue's profile. She'd had her eyes closed for the past thirty minutes, but she didn't fool him. The pretense of sleep had allowed her to avoid conversation with him. Maybe she'd just shut down, unable to process any more of the information coming at her from all directions.

She'd escaped a kidnapping a few months ago, had just been suspended from her job, narrowly missed another abduction from the bar last night, had been held at gunpoint this morning and had literally just dodged a bullet this afternoon. She deserved the downtime.

He sucked it up, turned on the radio and drove back to DC Metro content with his own thoughts for company.

When he swung into the valet parking area of the hotel, he nudged Sue's arm. "We're here."

She blinked and stretched, putting on a good show. "That went fast."

"I almost didn't want to wake you up."

"Oh." Her cheeks turned pink. "I wasn't really sleeping. Just recharging."

Two valets opened their doors at the same instant, and Hunter plucked the ticket from his guy's fingers and went around to Sue's side of the car. "Are you sure you're feeling all right?"

"I'm good." She stretched her arms in front of her, flipping her hands up and down. "Look, no visible scratches."

"It's a miracle we got out of that." He rested his fingertips on the small of her back. "When we get up to the room, I'm going to start putting some of this information together."

"We don't have much."

"It's more than Denver has right now."

They swept into the hotel and made it back to their room without incident.

Hunter opened the door cautiously, his gaze scanning the room. "Everything's just as we left it."

"That doesn't always mean it's safe."

"Spoken like a true spook." The door slammed behind them and Hunter threw the top lock. He stood in the middle of the room, hands on his hips, turning in a circle.

Sue threw herself across the bed and buried her chin in her palm. "What are you doing? Planning a remodel?"

"I wish I could repaper these walls."

"Huh?" She widened her eyes, blinking her lashes.

He spread out his hands. "I'd like to tack up the pictures and info we have so far and start making some connections, but I don't think the hotel would appreciate it."

"Whiteboard?"

"I think I'm just gonna have to go digital and create a file on my laptop. I can scan in the pictures we have, add the barbershop, the incidents, and put you and Denver at the top of it all. I'll even add your kidnapping and his setup."

"You're so sure he and I are linked?"

"He is." He flipped open his laptop. "That's all I need."

"Do you want my help over there, or are you better on your own?" She rolled onto her back and crossed her arms behind her head.

"You know what you can do?"

"What?"

"Get back to work on the phone we took off that guy this morning."

"None of my tricks worked earlier, and I'm worried about turning it on. He probably knows we have the phone and they can ping it for our location."

"I get it, but information from that phone could be invaluable." Hunter started a new file and entered Major Denver's name at the top on one side and Sue's name on the other. "Maybe we can try it when we're not at the hotel, and then move on to another location—keep 'em guessing."

"That's an idea." She wiggled her fingers at him. "You keep going. I'm going to make a few phone calls downstairs."

His head jerked up. "I'll be quiet."

"It's not that—CIA business." She shrugged and left the room, her phone cupped in her hand.

Hunter stared at the door for a few seconds after Sue clicked it shut behind her, then returned to his file.

By the time Sue returned to the room, he had all his actors set up in his file and crooked his finger in the air. "Have a look at this and let me know what you think."

The slamming of the bathroom door answered him and he spun around in his chair and called out, "Are you all right?"

"Fine. I'll be right out."

Several minutes later, she emerged patting her face dry with a towel. "How's it going?"

"It's going." He shoved his laptop in front of the empty chair at the desk and kicked out the chair with his foot. "Have a look."

She shuffled toward him, the towel still covering her face. Whipping it off, she plopped into the chair.

Drawing his brows over his nose, he studied her makeup-free face and the red tip of her nose. "Bad news from the Agency?"

"Just that they don't know when they're going to lift the suspension." She draped the towel over her shoulder. "Show me what you've done."

He got out of his chair and leaned over her shoulder, inhaling the soapy scent from her skin. With her hair over one shoulder, the back of her neck exposed damp tendrils of her hair.

His fingers itched to run the pad of his thumb over the soft strands. He reached past her and jabbed his finger at the display. "You and Denver are at the top, with the inciting incident right beneath you."

"The point when Denver went AWOL and my kidnapping in Istanbul."

"Right." He trailed his finger down the screen. "Then we have Pazir, Denver's contact in Afghanistan. The group that grabbed you, Jeffrey and Mason. The gunman whose phone we have. The barbershop. And the two men in the truck."

"What are your initial thoughts? You have to have more than Denver's belief that the guys who snatched me are connected to the group he was investigating before he was set up."

"Denver's word goes a long way with me." He

dragged himself away from her realm and sat back down in his own chair. "And then there's the timing. As soon as Denver makes contact with me to look you up, all these events occur."

"So, your presence here in DC is the trigger and I can blame you for everything?" She began typing on the keyboard.

"What are you entering?"

"My suspension from the CIA. Don't forget." She tapped a key with a flourish and spun the laptop around to face him. "That was in the works before you got here."

"Your abduction prompted that, didn't it?"

"Correction." She held up one finger. "Some bogus emails prompted that."

"Just like for Denver—emails to the CIA." Hunter scratched his chin. "I think someone may have hacked into the CIA's computer system, unless it's someone on the inside."

"It could be both." She stretched out her long legs, crossing them at the ankles. "The only entity I know even remotely capable of that is Dreadworm, but those hackers are not in the game of setting up people."

"We don't know that. They're in it to cause trouble."

"I thought they were in it to shed the light of truth on some dark corners of the government."

He raised his eyebrows. "You sound like a convert."

"I just don't think Dreadworm is responsible for

the content of those emails, even if they may have been the conduit." She wound her hair around her hand. "Do you want something to eat? I have to go out anyway to run a few errands, and I can pick up something and bring it back to the room, unless you want to order room service."

Hunter's pulse ticked up a few notches, but he schooled his face into an impassive mask. "Pizza? Chinese? Whatever's easy for you to carry out. Do you need my rental car?"

"No, thanks." She waved her hand. "I can walk."

"Are you sure it's safe out there for you?" She would expect him to ask that, wouldn't she?

"I have my weapon, and I'll take it with me." She tossed her hair over one shoulder and pushed back from the desk. "I—I won't be too long."

"Keep me posted. You should be okay. I don't think they tracked us to this hotel, so nobody would be following you from here."

"Exactly." She grabbed her purse from the bed and hitched it over her shoulder. "Do you trust me on the food?"

"Yeah...on the food."

The hotel door slammed before the last words left his lips—and maybe that was a good thing.

He waited two beats before springing from his chair and grabbing a gray hoodie from the closet. He stuffed his arms into it and zipped it up. Yanking up the bottom of the sweatshirt, he snapped his fanny pack containing his gun around his waist.

He gave the room a last look before slipping into

the hallway and heading for the stairwell. He jogged down the nine flights of stairs and peeked through a crack in the fire door, watching the lobby.

He spotted Sue's long stride across the floor, flipped up his hood and edged through the door. He fell in behind her as she exited the hotel, keeping out of sight.

He might trust Sue Chandler with picking out dinner, but that was about the extent of it.

She'd been hiding something from him since the minute she woke up in his hotel room—and he was about to find out what it was.

Chapter Seven

Sue took a quick glance over her shoulder before slipping into the ride-share car she'd ordered on her phone.

Leaning forward in her seat, she asked, "You have the address, right?"

"I know where the park is."

On cue, his GPS spit out the first direction, and the driver pulled away from the curb.

Sue pressed her hands on her bouncing knees. If they needed to talk to her, she'd have to pretend she had no problem meeting with them. Regaining their trust had to be her first step.

She didn't know how she'd lost that trust in the first place. Did they already know Hunter Mancini was in DC and why? Could she help it if the guy rescued her?

She fished her latest burner phone from a pocket hidden inside her purse and placed a call to The Falcon. His phone rang and rang and rang.

She'd have to do this on her own. She could brief

The Falcon later. Surely, he'd agree that she had to make this move.

She could be back at the hotel, Chinese food in hand, within an hour, with Hunter none the wiser.

Collapsing against the back seat, she covered her eyes with one hand. Why couldn't she have had the good luck to have met Hunter under normal circumstances? Why couldn't he be a DC doctor? An animal trainer? A ditchdigger?

She'd take any of those over what he was—a Delta Force soldier and a man on a mission.

She ran a hand beneath her nose and straightened her shoulders. She just had to convince Hunter her circumstances had nothing to do with Major Denver's and get him out of her life again…out of Drake's.

Hearing her son's voice tonight had given her strength. She had to do this for him—just as she'd always done everything for him the moment she found out she was pregnant.

"Where do you want me to drop you?" The driver met her eyes in the rearview mirror.

"The road nearest the band shell."

"There's a concert tonight?"

"I'm meeting a bird-watching group there." Not that she owed her driver an explanation of why she wanted to be dropped off near the band shell at Creek Run Park, but she didn't like leaving loose ends—like Hunter Mancini.

The driver pulled over on one of the park's access roads, and she cranked open the back door. "Thanks."

"Be careful out there."

She slammed the door and placed her hand on the outside pocket of her purse that concealed her weapon, putting her one Velcro rip between her hand and the cold metal of her gun.

Another car drove by on the access road, and she held her breath but it kept going. She crept forward on the path that led to the band shell.

Voices echoed from the stage and she drew up behind a tree and peered around the trunk at the band shell.

Clutches of kids...high school kids...were scattered across the stage practicing dance moves or projecting their voices into the night air. A teacher or director shouted instructions from the seats.

She eased out a breath. At least she wouldn't be meeting her contact in a deserted place in the park—unless he led her away from the lights and action.

A twig cracked behind her and she spun around, a gasp on her lips.

"Shh." Jeffrey, in the flesh, held up his hand. "It's just me."

"Yeah, that's why I'm freaked out." She wedged a hand on her hip and widened her stance. "Why the hell did you try to drug me last night and then send some goon to take me by force?"

"Who's your companion?" Jeffrey slid a hand into the pocket of his jacket.

"M-my companion?"

Jeffrey tilted his head to the side with a quick jerk. "Let's walk."

Her tennis shoes squished the mulch beneath her feet, damp with night dew, as Jeffrey took her arm.

She resisted the urge to shake off the pincerlike hold he had on her arm, advancing their status as comrades, two people on the same side.

He led her down a path, away from the performing teens, away from the comfort their voices brought. As she started to turn around, he shoved her against a tree and yanked her purse from her arm.

"Hey!" She spun around and made a grab for it, but he held it out of her reach and she didn't want to jump up and down to get it back.

"Do you have a weapon?"

She swallowed. "Of course I do."

He tossed her purse under a bush, several feet away. "Your companion?"

"That guy in the hotel room? He's a friend, an ex-boyfriend." She didn't want to stray too far from the truth. "He followed me and my friend out that night, saw me flailing around in the gutter after you slipped me the mickey and took me back to his hotel."

"If he's an ex, why does he have a hotel room and not a place of his own?" His dark eyes glittered through slits.

She rubbed her stinging palms together, dislodging bits of bark. "He doesn't live in DC. What does he matter, anyway? Why are you guys trying to bring me in by drugging me and holding me at gunpoint? You don't have to put on an act…unless you think someone is watching me here."

The pressure in her chest eased as she blew out

a breath. Maybe that was it. They knew she'd been suspended and figured the Agency was watching her. Maybe the assaults were just another staged kidnapping like the one in Istanbul.

"The CIA has suspended you." He pointed a finger at her. "Do they know?"

"Know about us? No." She folded her arms, pressing them against her chest. "Just more follow-up from Istanbul. Is that what this is all about? You think the CIA is onto me?"

A bird chirped from the darkness and stirred some leaves with its night flight.

Jeffrey held a finger to his lips and cocked his head. Then he took the same finger and sliced it across his throat. "If they make you, you're no longer of any use to us."

"Obviously." She straightened her spine against the chill making its way up her back. "That's not what happened. They don't have a clue. Do you think I'd do anything to jeopardize what we have going?"

"How do I know you're not bugged right now?" He waved a hand up and down her body.

She spread her arms out to the sides. "You're welcome to check. I initiated this meeting because I wanted to know why you were trying to take me by force. Do you really think I'd meet with you to try to entrap you?"

Clamping a hand on her shoulder, he forced her to face the tree and shoved her against it again.

The rough trunk bit into her palms again and she sucked in her bottom lip as Jeffrey reached under her shirt and thrust one hand between her breasts. She held her breath as his hands continued their impassionate but thorough search of her body. Thank God she hadn't decided to go rogue and show up with a listening or tracking device.

The Falcon had always given her explicit instructions to show up to meetings clean...but she hadn't been able to reach The Falcon. In fact, he hadn't given her an opportunity to even tell him about her suspension, which made her think he might be behind it.

Jeffrey's strong hands spun her around. "You've made it easy for us. You're coming with me."

"What do you mean? Where are you taking me?" This time she *did* shrug out of his grasp. "I can't just disappear from my life. It's one thing to do that in Istanbul, but it's not happening in DC."

He whipped his gun from his pocket and jabbed her in the ribs. "It's not up to you. We own you."

"I told you. Everything's on track. The CIA doesn't suspect a thing. I haven't been suspended because they're suspicious about any of my activity. That's all you need to know." She wrapped her fingers around the barrel of his gun. "I'll be delivering another piece of information soon."

"You don't get it." He put his face so close to hers she could smell the garlic on his breath. "We don't trust you anymore."

"That's ridiculous. I haven't given you any reason not to. The suspension is not my fault." Her knees began to buckle beneath her, but she widened her stance. Now was not the time to crumble. If she couldn't convince Jeffrey of her loyalty to the cause, he'd take her away and then the interrogation would begin...for real.

"Barbershop." He spat out the word between clenched teeth. "What were you doing at the barbershop? Did you think nobody would recognize you there?"

"I was hoping you would. I was reaching out and Rahid had mentioned the shop at our last meeting in Istanbul. I didn't expect you to try to run us off the road."

"If you knew that was us, why'd you pull a gun?" He nudged her again with his weapon.

"I was with my friend. He doesn't know anything about any of this."

"And then you contacted us with the phone you took off...our guy in the hotel room. Why didn't you do that before the barbershop?"

Sue swallowed. "I couldn't access the phone before. It took me a while to break into it. Give me another assignment. Let me prove myself."

Jeffrey kicked at a rock in the dirt. "This is not what we had in mind for an interrogation. You're coming with me—now."

He shoved her away from him with one hand, while he kept the gun trained on her with the other.

She stumbled and fell to her hands and knees. A wild thought came into her head to scramble for her purse and get her weapon.

A second later, Jeffrey grunted and crashed onto the ground next to her.

She twisted around and growled at Hunter looming above her, "What the hell are you doing? You just signed my death warrant."

Chapter Eight

"Not now." Hunter crouched beside the man he'd knocked out, the man who'd been threatening Sue, and searched his pockets. He had nothing on him, not even a phone.

Hunter pocketed the man's gun and reached down to grab Sue by the arm. "Let's get out of here before his backup arrives. He must have someone waiting in a getaway car."

Sue threw him off and launched to her feet. "Didn't you hear what I said? If I escape now, they're gonna kill me."

"They were going to kill you, anyway. Don't make me drag you out of here by force—because I will to save your damn life."

She blinked at him, brushed off her jeans and stomped past him. She stopped several feet in front of him and spun around. "Don't kill him, for God's sake."

"I have no intention of killing anyone." He spread his hands in front of him. "But let's get out of here before I *do* have to kill someone."

They tromped down the access road in silence, both breathing heavily. He didn't know what the hell Sue was involved in, but it was putting her in danger and he wasn't going to stand by and watch her get man-handled...or worse.

When they reached the sidewalk bordering the park, Hunter pulled out his phone and ordered a car from the same app that got him here.

Fifteen minutes later, Sue finally broke her silence when they pulled up to an Italian restaurant in Georgetown, not far from her place. "What are you doing?"

"I'm going to eat. I was starving waiting for you to come back with food. I'm also going to conduct my own interrogation—but you'll like mine a lot better than the one you were facing."

Her lips twisted as she got out of the car. "You wanna bet?"

He opened the door for her and the whoosh of warm garlic scent that greeted them made him feel almost comforted. He couldn't help it. The smells of Grandma Mancini's family dinners lived deep in his soul.

He raised two fingers at the hostess scurrying to greet him. "Table for two, please."

She seated them at a cozy, candlelit table with a checkered tablecloth, obviously laboring under some false impression.

Hunter waited until they'd ordered their food and a bottle of Chianti and a basket of garlic bread sat between them on the table before hunching forward on his elbows and saying, "Now, you're going to tell me what the hell is going on."

She plucked a piece of bread from the basket and ripped it in two. "I can't. It's top secret, and I'm not even kidding you."

"I know it's top secret. You wouldn't be meeting with a terrorist in the park in the middle of the night if it weren't. But, hey, you can tell me anything. I happen to have a top secret clearance."

He poured two glasses of wine from the bottle encased in wicker and held one out to her.

She dropped the bread onto a plate and took the glass by its stem. She tipped it at his. "Here's to top secret clearance."

He tapped her glass and took a long swig, the red wine warming his throat.

After taking a dainty sip from her own glass, Sue cupped the bowl with one hand. "What did you overhear?"

"Enough to know you're working with Jeffrey and his cohorts. For whom and how deep is something I aim to discover."

"Why can't you just leave it? Just know that I'm doing my job."

"I can't ignore it. I know it has something to do with Major Denver...and it looks like your assignment has gone haywire and you're in danger. I can't allow that to happen."

"Why is that?" Sue traced the rim of her wine glass with the tip of her finger.

He snatched her hand and squeezed her fingers

together. "You know damn well why. I wasn't the one who slipped out of that Paris hotel room in the early morning hours. I wasn't the one who ended our whirlwind affair. I never would've ended it. Those few weeks with you…"

He dropped her hand and gulped back the rest of his wine.

"I—I didn't realize…" Her cheeks flushed the same color as the wine.

"That I'd fallen so hard, so fast?" He snorted. "I thought I'd made enough of a fool of myself for you to figure that out."

"You were just coming out of a marriage—a bad marriage. I figured I was the rebound girl." Her dark eyes glowed in the soft light, making her look nothing like a rebound girl.

"The first couple of days I would've agreed with you, but the more time I spent with you…" He broke off. He was *not* going to open himself up to her again. "Look, I wanna keep you safe. It's the only way I'm going to find out how your group is connected to Denver."

Sue pursed her full lips and nodded. "My cover has probably already been blown. I'm not sure it matters anymore."

They stopped talking when the waitress arrived with their steaming plates of food. She looked up after she sprinkled some grated Parmesan on their pasta. "Can I get you anything else?"

Hunter raised his eyebrows at Sue, who answered no, and he shook his head.

He plunged his fork into his linguine. "I have a question."

"Of course you do."

"Did the Agency suspend you so that you could go deeper undercover with this group?"

"Before I answer that—" she directed the tines of her fork, dripping with tomato sauce, at him "—why did you follow me tonight? How did you know?"

"Lots of little things that added up to a great big thing—your reluctance to work on that phone when it could've been a treasure trove of information, your quick ID of the man in the photo with Jeffrey, even though the CIA didn't have a name for him." He shrugged. "The feeling ever since I got here that you've been keeping something from me."

Dropping her lashes over her eyes, she balanced her fork on the edge of the plate. "Then to answer your question, the CIA *did not* suspend me to allow me deeper access to this group. The CIA doesn't know about this group and doesn't know I'm working with them."

Hunter coughed, almost choking on his pasta. "Who are you working for if not the Agency?"

"It *is* the Agency—they just don't know about it."

"Black ops? Deep undercover?"

"That's right." Sue's shoulders dropped and she stuffed a large forkful of food into her mouth, closing her eyes as she chewed.

"It looks like a big weight just slipped off your shoulders." He cocked his head. "Have you ever told anyone that before? Does anyone know?"

"My dad."

Hunter steepled his fingers, resting his chin on the tips. Sue had told him about her father, the retired spook who had encouraged his daughter to follow in his footsteps, once she'd shown an affinity for languages and martial arts. Hunter wasn't sure he'd urge any daughter—or son—of his to enter the high-stakes and dangerous game of spying, but Sue had taken to it with a flair.

Not that he had children to urge one way or another—his ex had decided, after they were already married, she didn't want any. Julia must've known before he did that their marriage didn't stand a chance.

"He must be proud of you."

"I'm not sure about that." She pushed away her plate and folded her arms on the table.

"You're kidding, right? It's what he wanted for you from the beginning—not only a CIA agent but a double agent, someone working in the bowels of the machinery."

She dug her fingertips into her forearms. "I'm not sure I did things the way he would've wanted me to."

"It's crazy the amount of pressure we allow our families to exert on us." He reached around his own plate and brushed his fingers across the back of her hand. "I'm sure your father thinks the world of what you're doing."

"I've got a bigger problem now, don't I?" She uncrossed her arms, dislodging his hand, and picked up her wine glass, swirling the remnants of the Chianti.

"My contacts within this terrorist cell don't trust me anymore—and they're planning to take me captive to interrogate me."

"What about your first kidnapping?" Hunter leaned back in his chair and flagged down their passing waitress. "Check, please."

"What about it?"

"That wasn't real, was it? That was a preplanned meeting with your contacts."

"Ah, you don't believe I escaped, either."

He drilled his finger into the tabletop. "I'm convinced you know how to look after yourself, but it makes sense now. You orchestrated a kidnapping with them to make things look good on your side of the fence. Am I right?"

"You are." Sue whipped the napkin from her lap and dropped it onto the table next to her plate. "But now they want to kidnap me for real, and this time I don't think they're gonna offer me tea and cakes."

"How long have you been working undercover?"

"Over four years now."

Hunter rolled his eyes to the ceiling and counted on his fingers. "You were doing this when we met in Paris."

"I was."

He dropped his gaze to her face. "Is that why…? Never mind."

He snatched up the check the waitress dropped off and reached for his wallet. "You're going to need some protection."

"I thought I had it." She leveled a finger at him.

"You dropped poor Jeffrey before he even knew what hit him."

"I mean someone official, someone at the Agency."

"I don't have anyone at the Agency—just my contact. The person who recruited and trained me. He's the only one, as far as I know, who knows what I'm doing. In fact—" she slid her jacket from the back of her chair "—I believe I'm on suspension for the very activities I've been doing undercover, only the CIA doesn't know I'm undercover."

"That's a dangerous game, Sue." He couldn't help the way his heart jumped at the thought of Sue in the middle of all this intrigue—even though he knew better, knew she could handle herself. "You need to contact him right away."

"I tried earlier through our regular channels, and he's not picking up."

"But this has hit critical mass now." He smacked his fist into his palm.

"You don't need to tell me that, although I may have figured a way out, a way to keep working this group."

He raised one eyebrow. He hadn't intended on coming out here and playing bodyguard to a badass spy, who was way more hooked in than he realized, but she'd just pushed his protective instincts into overdrive. "You don't need to keep working with this group. Call it a day and fold your hand."

"This is almost five years of work, Hunter. You don't give up on five years of blood, sweat and tears—and sacrifices. You wouldn't. You can't even give up on Denver. You won't give up on Denver." She shrugged into her jacket and flipped her hair out of the neckline. "Don't tell me what to do."

He held up his hands. Where had he heard that before? "What's your plan?"

"I'll run it past my contact first, but since Jeffrey never saw what hit him and I was just about to go off with him, I can make the case that you followed me without my knowledge—which you did—and were just playing the protective boyfriend."

"Which I was." He felt heat prickles on his neck. "Except for the boyfriend part."

She ignored him.

"I can arrange another meeting for them to pick me up."

"No!" The word was out of his mouth before his brain could stop it. He coughed. "I mean, they're not going to believe you and you know what's waiting for you on the other side of a so-called meeting with these guys. They're gonna want to make you talk and they'll use any means necessary. You know that, Sue."

She lifted her shoulders. "I have to try to salvage my mission."

"Wait and see what your contact has to say. I can't believe he'd be willing to sacrifice an asset like you for a compromised mission."

"I have my burner phone back at the hotel." She jerked a thumb over her shoulder. "I'll try to call him again when we get back."

Hunter had to keep his fingers crossed that this

guy was reasonable and would see the futility in having Sue continue with a group that clearly didn't trust her anymore.

Through all this, he couldn't deny that Sue's position gave her an even better perspective on the web entangling Denver—the same web had her in its sticky strands.

"Let's go, then." He added a few more bucks to his cash on the tray for the tip and pushed back from the table.

When they stepped outside, Sue huddled into her jacket. "The hotel's not far. We can catch the Metro."

"No way." He held out his phone. "I already ordered a car."

As they waited, he rubbed her back. "We don't have to figure this all out here in DC. You're suspended. The Agency doesn't expect you to sit around waiting for them to call you back. We can get out of here, someplace safer for you."

"I need to stay right here. Besides, where would we go?"

"We could go to my place."

She twisted her head to the side. "Colorado?"

The fact that she remembered where he lived caused his mouth to slant upward in a ridiculous smile. "Clean air, wildflowers for days and mountain views for miles."

"I really can't leave DC, Hunter. It's impossible." She waved at the approaching sedan. "This is our guy, right?"

"Yeah." He lunged forward to get the door for her.

"Why are you so wedded to DC? You don't even have family here, right? Dad, mom and sister's family all in South Carolina?"

Sue tripped getting into the car and grabbed onto the door. "Good memory. Yes, but I have things to do here."

Good memory? She had no idea the things he remembered about her—the way her brown eyes sparkled when she laughed, the curve of her hip, the hitch in her breath when he entered her.

"Are you getting in or planning to push the car?"

Hunter blinked and ducked, joining her in the back seat. They kept their mouths shut during the brief ride back to the hotel, but once outside the car they both started talking at once.

Tucking her hand in the crook of his arm, she leaned her chin against his shoulder. "There's no use trying to talk me out of anything, Hunter, until I contact The Falcon."

"The Falcon?"

"That's his code name—and I've never told anyone that before."

"Does that mean you're ready to trust me now? Tell me what the two of you have been busy infiltrating all these years?"

She pressed a finger to her lips as they got into the elevator with another couple.

Hunter shifted from foot to foot on the ride up to their floor.

When they got to the room, Sue made a beeline to the hotel safe in the closet. She crouched in front of it and entered the code she'd plugged in earlier. Cupping the phone in her hand, she sat on the edge of the bed with a bounce.

"You just call each other on cell phones?" He sat beside her and the mattress dipped, her body slanting slightly toward his.

She scooted forward to straighten up. "It's a little more complicated than that."

She tapped the display to enter the number and held the phone to her ear. A few seconds later, her body became rigid and she sucked in a quick breath.

Hunter watched her face, as her brows collided over her nose.

"Two, eight, three, five, six." She spit out the numbers in rapid succession.

She jumped to her feet and repeated. "Two, eight, three, five, six."

The phone slid from her hand and she spun around to face him. "He's gone. The Falcon has been compromised."

Chapter Nine

She paced to the window, twisting her fingers in front of her. She chanted under her breath, "This is bad. This is bad."

"How do you know? What just went down?" Hunter leaned forward and scooped the burner phone from the floor. "Was that a code between the two of you?"

"We have a number code that changes for each phone call. We answer calls from each other with random numbers, and the caller returns with the appropriate sequence of numbers based on the original set. It's a calculation The Falcon made up. Nobody knows it but us." She clasped the back of her neck beneath her hair and squeezed.

"What happened this time?" Hunter retrieved a bottle of water from the minifridge and handed it to her.

"When I placed the call, someone said hello with the voice alteration program on. We're not supposed to answer with a hello, but I guess he could've slipped up."

"You've never even heard The Falcon's real voice?"

She shook her head and her hair whipped back and forth across her face. "I have no idea who he is or where he resides—or who else works on the team."

"He answered hello and you threw a random code at him, right?"

"Yes, but he couldn't respond. He paused. He recited some numbers, but I knew by then I didn't have The Falcon on the other end of the line." She pressed two fingers to her right temple. "I don't know what could've happened."

"Maybe he lost the phone and some random person picked it up and was fooling around."

Digging her fist into her side, she tilted her head. "I know you're trying to make me feel better, Hunter, but just stop. We both know something's wrong. Jeffrey tried to take me in for questioning and now this."

"They could've stolen the phone off him, trying to find another way to reach you."

"How do they know The Falcon? *I* don't even know The Falcon."

The thought of The Falcon, her lifeline, disappearing from the other end of that burner phone suddenly hit her like a sledgehammer and she collapsed onto the bed before her knees gave out beneath her. She flung herself facedown on the mattress and stared at the comforter inches from her nose. "M-maybe The Falcon figured we were made and dropped out of sight for a while."

The bed sagged as Hunter sat beside her. "Sure, that could be it. If he's running a black ops organization, the guy has skills. He's gonna lay low until it's safe for him to poke up his head."

"The timing couldn't be worse. I'm under suspicion at work, and I always thought The Falcon would be able to rescue me if things got too heated. Someone in his position would be able to tell the investigators to back off." She buried her face in the crook of her arm. "What if the CIA actually believes I've been working with this terrorist group and there's no Falcon to bail me out?"

"It's going to be okay, Sue. We're going to clear you and Denver at the same time." He squeezed her shoulder. "But you have to help me out. You have to give me something—something more than fake kidnappings and barbershops and shadowy black ops commanders. I wanna know what you know."

She squeezed her eyes shut. Should she really tell Hunter what she knew? If she told him her biggest secret, he might walk away from her forever. Last night she would've welcomed that prospect, but now? She'd found her shoulder to lean on.

Rolling onto her back, she sighed. "The group we've infiltrated has ties all over the world. That's why the people I met in Istanbul are connected to a cell here in DC. In the past years, we've become aware that they're planning something big here in the US, but they're being coy."

"This group has tentacles in Afghanistan? Syria? Nigeria?"

"Yes, yes and yes." She narrowed her eyes. Hunter

knew more than she thought. "Why did you mention those places?"

"Because Denver has been tied to all those places, as well—he was placed at a bombing at a Syrian refugee center, he was inspecting suspicious arms at an embassy outpost in Nigeria and he went AWOL in Afghanistan—and some believe he's still there."

"It sounds like he's tied into the same structure. Who does he know in Afghanistan? Who was his contact there? Do you know?"

"Pazir—that's the only name I have."

Sue drew her bottom lip between her teeth. "I don't know that name, but I'm going to do a little research tomorrow."

"Thatta girl. Let's meet this thing head-on and be proactive. No point in sitting around waiting for things to happen."

She rolled off the bed and stamped her feet on the carpeted floor. "You mean like intruders, car chases and abductions?"

"Exactly." Hunter formed his fingers into a gun and pointed at her.

"Where's Jeffrey's gun?"

"In my jacket pocket. I'll lock it up in the safe if there's room. In a day or two, I might have as many guns as you do cell phones." He plucked his jacket from the back of a chair. "What did you get off that phone?"

"The number to set up that meeting tonight."

"What did you hope to accomplish by sneaking away to the park to meet with Jeffrey?"

"The chance to convince them that I'm still on their side, maybe persuade them to stop attacking me." She yawned, a heavy lethargy stealing over her body. "Can we pick this up tomorrow? I'm going to brush my teeth and hit the sack."

"We'll be thinking more clearly in the morning, anyway." He grabbed a couple of pillows from the bed and tossed them onto the sofa. "You take the bed, and I'll stretch out over here."

She eyed the sofa, wrinkling her nose. "You're not going to be stretching out on that, Hunter." She patted the bed. "This is big enough for both of us."

His gaze shifted to the bed and his Adam's apple bobbed in his throat. "I don't want to crowd you... or make you uncomfortable."

"It's not like we haven't shared a bed before."

"Yeah, but we weren't sleeping in *that* bed." He thrust out a hand. "Sorry, had to put that out there."

She grinned, a punch-drunk laugh bubbling to her lips. "Oh, I remember."

She turned her back on him and weaved her way to the bathroom to escape the intensity of those blue eyes. When she'd safely parked herself in front of the sink, she hunched over the vanity and stared at her flushed cheeks.

Must be the Chianti...and the fear. Sharing a bed with Hunter Mancini was a dangerous proposition—no telling where that pillow talk might lead.

She brushed her teeth, wound her hair into a pony-tail and washed her face. If he were as exhausted as she was, he'd be out already.

Opening the bathroom door, she peered into the room, spying Hunter in front of the room safe.

He twisted his head around. "You wanna share the combination with me, so I can lock up my weapon collection?"

She reeled off the numbers. "Bathroom's all yours. I'm ready to black out."

Once he secured the guns in the safe, Hunter stepped into the bathroom and closed the door behind him.

Sue let out a breath and stripped out of her clothes in record time. She pulled on a pair of pajama bottoms and a camisole and crawled between the covers.

Hunter had already turned off all the lights except for one over the bed. Sue reached over and flicked it off, leaving the flickering blue light from the TV as the only illumination in the room.

When the bathroom door clicked open, she squeezed her eyes closed and then relaxed her face muscles. She deepened her breathing. As long as she pretended to be asleep, she'd be safe from Hunter…or rather her own desire for him. She'd always be safe with Hunter. She'd known that from the moment she met him in Paris.

He'd been wounded by his ex. She'd cheated on him while he'd been deployed, and Sue's heart ached knowing she'd added to his love battle scars.

Her lashes fluttered and she watched him undress through the slits in her eyes. The glow from the TV highlighted the flat planes and smooth muscle of his body.

He'd stripped to his boxers, and she held her breath as he crossed the room to his suitcase in the corner. He glanced over his shoulder once, then plunged his hand into his bag, dragging out a pair of gym shorts—as if those could hide the beauty of his body and dampen the temptation that coursed through her veins at the sight of him.

He crept past the foot of the bed and tugged at the covers behind her. The bed squeaked as he eased into it.

The mattress bounced a little and it sounded like he was punching pillows. Then the TV station changed from the news to a cooking show, and every muscle in Sue's body seized up.

She'd been hoping he'd fall into an exhausted sleep, but no. The man had more energy than Drake high on sugar at a bouncy house birthday party.

She covered her mouth. She'd been avoiding making those comparisons between her son and Hunter.

A soft whisper floated over her. "Is the TV keeping you awake? I'll turn it down."

"I'm sorry, Hunter."

"Don't worry about it. I can watch the cooking shows without sound—unless it's the light that's bothering you."

She turned toward him, pulling the covers to her chin. "No, I meant I'm sorry that I left you in Paris like that."

He lifted one bare shoulder, and the sheet slid from his chest, exposing his chiseled pecs. "It's all right, Sue. It was a fling—a totally hot, unforgettable fling—and I don't regret it, even though it ended the way it did."

"I—I always meant to look you up later."

"Don't." He lifted a lock of her hair and wrapped it around his finger. "You don't have to pretend."

"I wasn't pretending then—" she scooted closer to his warmth "—and I'm not pretending now."

A low light burned in his eyes, and it sent a shudder of anticipation through her body. She knew they'd wind up here together—the moment she woke up in the bed of his other hotel room. At the time, she didn't know how or where, but she knew she had to have this man again, regardless of the consequences.

His fingers crept through her hair until he loosened the band holding her ponytail together. He pulled it out and scooped one hand through her loose strands.

"As long as you want this now, I'm not even going to ask for a tomorrow."

She placed two fingers against his soft lips. "Let's not talk about tomorrow."

"Let's not talk." He slid down until they were face-to-face. He cupped her jaw and pressed his lips against hers. His tongue swept across the seam of her mouth, and she sucked it inside.

They hadn't even kissed since he'd walked back into her life, so this intimate invasion left her breathless. How many times had she dreamed about Hunter's kisses?

His soft lips carried an edge of greedy urgency, as if he couldn't get enough of her—or maybe he was taking what he could get before she disappeared from his life again.

And she'd have to disappear.

Without breaking his connection to her, he shifted his hands beneath her pajama top and caressed her aching breasts. Would he feel the difference in her body? The new softness since her pregnancy and the birth of Drake?

A sigh escaped her lips as he rolled her nipples between his fingertips. Men didn't notice things like that—even men like Hunter, who had a surprisingly tender side despite the rough edges.

She placed a hand on Hunter's hip, her fingers tucking inside the waistband of his boxers. Resting her forehead against his, she whispered against his mouth, "I've been waiting so long for this."

He turned his head to the side and growled in her ear. "Same. Never forgot you. Never wanted to forget you."

He slid his hands to her shoulders and pulled her camisole over her head. He dipped his head and let his tongue finish what his fingers started, teasing her nipples to throbbing peaks.

The tingling sensation curled in her belly and zigzagged down the insides of her thighs. She hooked a leg over his hip and rocked against him.

His hands slid into her pajama bottoms and her underwear at the same time and he caressed her derriere. He hissed between his teeth. "So smooth."

She yanked down his boxers and skimmed her hand down the length of his erection. "So smooth."

His breath hitched as he nibbled her earlobe. "Take those off."

"You don't have to ask me twice." She dragged his underwear over his muscled thighs and down the rest of his legs, dropping them onto the floor.

Before he asked, she stripped off her bottoms and tossed them over her shoulder. "Now we're even."

With a smile lifting one corner of his mouth, he encircled her waist with his hands and pulled her toward him.

He always did like her on top first. She straddled him and folded her body to smush her breasts against his chest as he dug his fingers into her bottom.

She laid a path of kisses from the curve of his shoulder to the side of his neck and his strong jaw. She gasped as his fingers probed the soft flesh between her legs.

As he rhythmically stroked her, she rocked against him, closing her eyes. The passion built from the tips of her toes and raced up her legs, pooling where his fingers teased her and then clawing through her belly.

She caught her breath and held it, every muscle in her body tensing, awaiting her release.

As her climax claimed every inch of her body, her lids flew open and her gaze met the flickering blue light in Hunter's eyes. He plunged his fingers inside her wet core and he rode out her orgasm with her, holding her gaze with his. She couldn't break that connection even if she wanted to—and she didn't want to.

Her body shook and trembled as she came down from her high only to have Hunter enter her slowly and deliberately. He steadied her movement by placing his hands on her hips, guiding her onto his erection as he thrust upward.

They hit their stride and she rode him hard, controlling how deep he went and how fast. He soon tired of her game.

Pinching her waist, he flipped her onto her back and wedged one hand against the headboard as he continued to plunge into her.

Her desire for him burned once again in her pores, and she wrapped her legs around his hips.

He stopped moving and his voice came out in a strangled whisper. "Are you close?"

"Don't wait for me. It feels like you're ready to explode."

"Waited for you for almost four years. I can wait."

His words sent a river of electric current across her flesh. She arched her back and undulated against him where their bodies met.

He sucked in his breath and braced his hands on either side of her head as he pressed and rubbed against her, his face tense, his jaw tight.

He was a man of steel.

She puffed out a breath, which started the avalanche. Her orgasm rolled through her, turning her muscles to jelly.

Feeling her release, Hunter picked up where he'd left off, driving into her, lifting her bottom off the mattress with the force of his thrusts.

He exploded inside her and kept pounding her until they both lay drained and exhausted.

Totally sated, Sue let out a squeak. "You're squishing me."

"I'm sorry." His body slid off hers, slick with sweat and boneless.

"I can't move."

He rolled his head to the side and opened one eye. "I can barely move."

"Water?"

"I thought you couldn't move?"

She snorted. "I'm afraid if I don't move now, I'll never get up from this bed."

Brushing his knuckles against her hip, he said, "That doesn't sound so bad to me right now. Here, we're in a bubble. Out there…"

"It's a whole different kind of bubble out there, but the night is young—sort of."

His eyebrows jumped. "You mean you're going to require more of me?"

"If you play your cards right." She smoothed her hand across his damp chest and rolled from the bed. "There's still water in the minibar, right?"

"I can get it."

She swept her camisole from the floor and pulled it over her head. "You stay right there and keep that bed warm."

"Impossible without you in it, and how come you look even sexier with that top on and your bare bottom peeking from the hem?"

"Because you have sex on the brain now." She

bent forward in front of the fridge to grab a bottle of water, mooning him.

"You don't play fair, woman." He threw a pillow at her but missed.

"I sure hope you have better aim with a gun than you do with a pillow." She spun around, holding out the bottle of water.

As Hunter grabbed another pillow to chuck at her, a soft knock at the hotel door had them both suspended, the look of shock on Hunter's face surely mirroring her own.

"Wait." He leaped from the bed, snagging his boxers from the floor.

She dropped the bottle of water onto the floor and crept toward the door, hugging the wall in case someone decided to shoot point-blank into the door.

The knock sounded again—louder, stronger.

Hunter appeared beside her, thrusting her behind him as he leaned to the side to peer through the peephole. "It's someone in a dark hoodie. I can't see his face. Too short to be Jeffrey."

A woman's voice called through the door. "The code. Give me a code, Nightingale."

Chapter Ten

Sue pressed a hand against her heart. "It must be someone working in The Falcon's unit. Maybe she brought news of The Falcon."

Hunter held up his hand. "Hang on."

As he turned to the safe in the closet, Sue called out. "One, five, two, two, seven."

The woman coughed and rested her forehead against the door, but she answered the correct sequence of responding numbers.

Hunter sidled up next to her with a gun pointed at the door.

"She's legit, Hunter. I'm opening the door."

"Slowly." He stood behind the door as she eased it open.

The woman fell against the door with a thump, and as Sue widened the door, the woman fell into the room, landing in a heap on the floor.

"Oh my God." Sue dropped to her knees beside the woman. "What's wrong?"

"I hope she wasn't followed here." Hunter poked

"FAST FIVE" READER SURVEY

Your participation entitles you to:
✳ 4 Thank-You Gifts Worth Over $20!

Complete the survey in minutes.

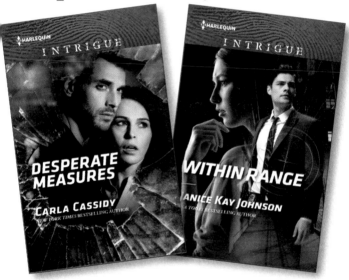

Get 2 FREE Books

Your Thank-You Gifts include **2 FREE BOOKS** and **2 MYSTERY GIFTS**. There's no obligation to purchase anything!

See inside for details.

Dear Reader,

Since you are a lover of our books, your opinions are important to us... and so is your time.

That's why we made sure your **"FAST FIVE" READER SURVEY** can be completed in just a few minutes. Your answers to the five questions will help us remain at the forefront of women's fiction.

And, as a thank-you for participating, we'd like to send you **4 FREE THANK-YOU GIFTS!**

Enjoy your gifts with our appreciation,

Pam Powers

To get your
4 FREE THANK-YOU GIFTS:

✳ Quickly complete the "Fast Five" Reader Survey
and return the insert.

"FAST FIVE" READER SURVEY

#		
1	Do you sometimes read a book a second or third time?	○ Yes ○ No
2	Do you often choose reading over other forms of entertainment such as television?	○ Yes ○ No
3	When you were a child, did someone regularly read aloud to you?	○ Yes ○ No
4	Do you sometimes take a book with you when you travel outside the home?	○ Yes ○ No
5	In addition to books, do you regularly read newspapers and magazines?	○ Yes ○ No

YES! I have completed the above Reader Survey. Please send me my 4 FREE GIFTS (gifts worth over $20 retail). I understand that I am under no obligation to buy anything, as explained on the back of this card.

❑ I prefer the regular-print edition
182/382 HDL GNTY

❑ I prefer the larger-print edition
199/399 HDL GNTY

FIRST NAME   LAST NAME

ADDRESS

APT.#   CITY

STATE/PROV.   ZIP/POSTAL CODE

HI-819-FF19

his head out the door and then shut it, throwing the top lock in place.

Sue had loosened the woman's sweatshirt and pushed the hoodie back from her head. She gasped and fell back on her heels. "She's been beaten."

Hunter crouched beside her. "What happened? Who did this?"

The woman's lashes fluttered and her slack mouth hung open, a trickle of blood seeping from the corner.

"I think she lost consciousness."

"Let's get her on the sofa. Get some towels." He slid his arms beneath the woman's small form and lifted her in a single motion.

As he carried her to the sofa, Sue pulled on her underwear and rushed to the bathroom to collect the extra towels. She grabbed a hand towel and ran it beneath the faucet.

Had The Falcon's entire unit been blown wide open? Were they all targets now?

When she returned to the room, Hunter was seated on the floor next to the sofa checking the woman's vitals.

"Is she still alive?"

"Barely." He peeled the woman's blouse back from her chest. "She has multiple wounds. These look like stab wounds."

"God, what happened to her?" Sue pressed a towel against the woman's bleeding head.

"The same thing that would've happened to you had you gone along with Jeffrey tonight."

Sue clenched her teeth as she used the wet towel to clean up some of the blood on the woman's face. "How did she get here?"

"God knows." Hunter clasped his hands behind his neck. "She needs medical attention, Sue. We can't do this here. We're losing her."

"If she wanted to go to the hospital, she would've gone to the hospital—she came here instead."

"Maybe just to warn you, and she's done that." He rose to his feet. "We have to get help. She's somebody's daughter, sister, wife, mother. My God, if this were you, I'd want immediate medical care for you, regardless of any other circumstances."

"Of course, you're right." She smoothed the corner of the towel across the woman's mouth. She might have a son, just like her.

"I'm calling 911, and then I'll call the front desk of the hotel. We can say we don't know her. She came up to our room like this, knocked on the door and collapsed. We don't know anything."

"Does she have ID? Did you check?"

"I didn't." He held up his phone. "You do that while I call."

Sue searched the woman's pockets and scanned the floor inside the room and in the hallway in case she'd dropped something.

When Hunter ended his call, Sue spread her hands. "Nothing. She has nothing."

Ten minutes later, Sue waved at the EMTs as they came off the elevator. "Over here. She's here."

For several chaotic minutes, the EMTs stabilized

the injured woman and got her onto a stretcher as the police questioned Sue and Hunter.

The questions continued even after the EMTs had taken away the patient, but Sue had years of lying under her belt and she maintained her ignorance without blinking an eye.

Maybe Hunter didn't have quite the same skills in mendacity as she possessed, but his military training had given him an erect bearing and poker face that was hard to pick apart.

In the end, the cops had no reason to believe she and Hunter had injured the woman or even knew who she was—and the hotel's CCTV would back them up.

Sue clicked the door closed behind the last of the police officers and braced her hands against it, hanging her head between her arms. "I wonder who she is."

"Hopefully, she'll regain consciousness and tell us…and tell us why she came here." Hunter traced a line down her curved spine. "She must've used every last ounce of her strength to get here and recite that code to you."

Sue turned and nestled her head against Hunter's chest, just because she could. "How did she know I was here? How did she even know about me? The Falcon has never even implied I was part of a group."

"Different plans for different people. Maybe you're the only CIA agent and The Falcon has different rules for you." He squeezed her shoulders. "Let's get back to bed for the remaining hours we have left in this morning."

"We're going to try to see her at the hospital tomorrow, right?"

"I don't see how we're ever going to get any information out of her if we don't—and I'm sure she wanted you to have info or she never would've shown up here." He leaned over her to put his eye to the peephole in the door. "I hope nobody followed her. We've been secure at this hotel so far."

"We *think* we have. How did she find us?"

Hunter yawned and flicked off the light in the entryway. "We'll ask her tomorrow."

On the way to the bed, Hunter peeled off the T-shirt he'd hastily thrown on when the EMTs arrived and stepped out of his jeans and boxers at the same time. He slid his naked body between the sheets and patted the bed beside him. "Has your name on it."

Sue shed her pajamas and underwear and crawled in beside him. She didn't know if she could do another round with Hunter, but if he wanted her again she wouldn't mind one bit—and she owed him.

Instead, he pulled her back against his front and draped an arm over her waist. He nuzzled the back of her neck. "Would you think I'm heartless if I told you I'm glad that wasn't you bloody and beaten, looking for refuge?"

"No. I know what you mean. You're not happy it happened to her, either, but...yeah." She threaded her fingers through his and planted a kiss on his palm. "I'm glad you're here, Hunter. I've never had a bodyguard before."

"I'm here and I'm not leaving."

She squeezed her eyes shut. *Don't be so sure about that, Hunter.*

THE FOLLOWING MORNING, Hunter slipped from the bed, careful not to disturb Sue. He'd lain awake most of the night as much to soak in feeling Sue's body next to his as to keep watch over her.

He crept to the bathroom and shut the door behind him.

He didn't like the fact that the woman had shown up at their hotel room, hanging on to consciousness by a thread. How did she know she hadn't been followed? She could've led her assailants right to Sue's doorstep.

Or maybe that's what she planned. Who knew where she learned that reciprocal code? Sue had no idea whether or not this woman was connected to The Falcon and the work they were doing.

He couldn't have left a battered woman in the hotel corridor anyway, but he didn't trust her. Hell, he still didn't trust Sue. He knew she'd been hiding something from him. Why not just come out and tell him she was a double agent, a mole embedded with a terrorist group? Why sneak around when they were on the same side...or at least he assumed they were.

Sue had told him she was black ops working for the other side, but what if she were just working for the other side? People turned all the time for money, ideology, revenge. The CIA seemed to have its suspicions.

If he were honest with himself, he didn't know much about Sue's work or life. He'd heard about the CIA father, the overbearing stepmother, the beloved sister. He hadn't fallen for her based on anything she'd told him about herself.

He'd gotten in deep because of the way she made him feel. Rebound. He turned his face to the spray of water in the shower.

He'd clicked with her so quickly because she was nothing like his ex-wife, Julia—except for the secrets and now the lies.

Sue had wanted him at a time when he'd no longer felt wanted. Powerful stuff to resist.

He shut off the water and snatched a towel from the rack next to the shower. Maybe this time, he needed to be the one to walk away—but not before he got everything he could about Major Denver out of her.

She could be lying about what she knew about Denver, too. Once you caught a woman in one lie, you never knew how many more could be on her lips.

The knock on the door caused him to drop his towel. "Did I wake you?"

"Just by not being in bed when I reached for you." Sue knocked on the door and jiggled the handle. "Have you gotten modest all of a sudden? I've seen it all, Mancini…and I'd like to see it again."

He left the towel on the floor and reached over to let her in.

The dark gaze that meandered over his body from head to toe felt like a caress. When she met his eyes, she licked her lips. "Thought we might shower together this morning."

He stepped back, whipped aside the shower curtain and turned on the water again. "Great idea."

As she joined him under the warm spray and he kissed her wet mouth, all his doubts disappeared... or rather receded into one small corner of his brain.

After breakfast in the hotel restaurant, Sue called the hospital, but once the nurse who answered the phone determined that Sue was not related to their visitor from last night, she refused to give her any information at all.

Sue shook her head at Hunter and raised her voice. "I'm the one who called 911. She stumbled to my hotel room."

A few seconds later, Sue slammed the phone to the table, rattling the silverware.

"No luck?"

"She refuses to tell me anything."

Hunter drained the coffee from his cup and clicked it back into the saucer. "If the nurse is that closemouthed, we don't stand much of a chance getting in there to talk to her, even if she does regain consciousness."

"The nurse wouldn't even tell me if she was awake or not." Sue broke a crust of toast in two and crumbled it between her fingers.

"I'm thinking not. If she used the last bit of energy she had to make it to our hotel and give you that code, I think she'd want to talk to you when she comes to."

"Maybe, maybe not, but there are ways to get into hospitals and see patients, whether you're family or not."

"Yeah, I almost forgot…you're CIA." He winked and pulled his laptop from its sleeve and placed it on the table. "You ready to look at everything I have on Denver?"

"Go for it." She raised her hand as the waitress walked by. "Can I get a refill on my coffee, please?"

Hunter brought up the spreadsheet and file he'd been populating since yesterday while Sue had been making her mysterious phone calls and attending her mysterious meetings with terrorists.

He swung the computer toward her. "You and Denver are at the top, and my goal is to connect you by the time we reach the bottom of the tree."

"Have his contacts told him about an impending attack on US soil, too?"

"Yes, that's what he believes is happening. The problem is that the attack is not being carried out by one group—or even the usual suspects. This group is scattered, has no defined leader—and may have connections to the US government."

Sue's heart skittered. "Traitors on the inside?"

"It's the only way to explain the setup of Denver. It's widespread and there seems to be no urgency to clear Denver's name, even when charges against him have been shown to be false."

Sue's phone buzzed on the table beside her, and she shot him a glance beneath knitted brows. "It's my manager."

"Are you going to answer it? Maybe you've been cleared to go back to work."

"I doubt it." She lifted the phone to her ear. "Hi, Ned."

She cocked her head as she listened to the voice on the other end of the line. "What are you doing on the sidewalk in front of my place? I'm not home, Ned."

Sue's eyes widened in her suddenly pale face, and Hunter's insides lurched.

"Okay, okay. I'm at the Hay-Adams in the coffee shop." She ended the call and tapped her chin with the edge of the phone. "Ned's coming over. He wants to talk to me."

Hunter swallowed. "He couldn't do it over the phone?"

"Apparently not."

"He just wants to update you." Hunter shrugged, feigning a nonchalance that didn't match the rumblings in his belly. He tapped his laptop's display. "Did the group you infiltrated ever mention weapons from Nigeria? Apparently, there was a secret stash there that Denver knew about or suspected."

"I'd have to retrieve all my notes, which I pretty much turned over to The Falcon."

"You kept copies?"

"I have copies of all my reports on my laptop. I can definitely go through them with you, and you can tag anything that relates to Major Denver."

They went through another cup of coffee each as they discussed Hunter's spreadsheet, and he really felt that they were making some progress. If they could get to the bottom of this plot and link it to Denver's findings before he went AWOL, the army would have no choice but to exonerate the major.

Sue had been keeping an eye on the entrance to the restaurant, and she lifted her hand and waved at a compact, balding African American man charging toward them.

When he reached their table, Sue stood up and pulled out the chair across from her. "Have a seat, Ned. This is Hunter Mancini. Hunter, Ned Tucker."

Hunter had risen from his chair and stuck out his hand to the other man.

Ned looked him up and down before releasing his grip and taking his seat. "Military?"

"Delta Force. You?"

"Air Force." Ned leveled a stubby finger at Sue. "Are you helping her out?"

"I'm trying. Why?"

"Because she needs it." Ned turned to Sue and covered one of her hands with his. "Sue, what have you been up to? There is no way I believe you've been spying for the other side, but I'm hearing about evidence against you that's giving me pause. Enlighten me."

"You enlighten me." Sue wiggled her fingers at the waitress. "Do you want some coffee, Ned?"

"I'm wired enough as it is." He turned to the approaching waitress and asked her for a glass of water. "I can't tell you much, Sue."

"Bogus emails again? Emailing classified documents?" She pinged her coffee cup. "None of that is true, Ned. It's been planted, just like those emails about Major Rex Denver were fakes."

"It's more than that, Sue." Ned glanced over his shoulder and ducked his head. "The investigators have pictures—pictures of you meeting with known terrorists."

Sue dropped her spoon onto the saucer with a clatter that further jangled Hunter's nerves. Those pictures could definitely be in existence, but who could've taken them?

"That's absurd. Any photos of me with terrorists would be meetings with informants."

Ned wiped his brow with a napkin and then crumpled it in his fist. "Okay, that makes sense, and any of those meetings would be documented as protocol dictates, right? Right, Sue?"

"Of course. Protocol."

"Speaking of protocol." Ned thanked the waitress for his water and downed half the glass in one gulp. "You never saw me here. We never had this conversation. I have my own sources within the Agency and someone gave me a heads-up, but if anyone found out I relayed this info to you, I'd be in almost as much trouble as you're in now."

"I appreciate you're going out on a limb for me, Ned. This is going to come to nothing, but even if it doesn't, I'll leave you out of it." She patted his arm. "Don't worry."

Ned raised one eyebrow to his bald pate. "You're always telling me that like you have some secret guardian angel. I hope you don't mean your old man, because as revered as he is in the Agency, not even he could get you out of this mess if it's true and you don't have the documentation to support those meetings."

"Don't worry." She slid a plate with a half-eaten pastry on it toward Ned. "Have a Danish."

"That's even worse." He patted his rounded belly. "My wife still has me on that diet."

"Thanks for the intel. We can handle it."

Ned rose from the table and said his goodbyes. Then he snatched the Danish from the plate and waved it in the air. "Now you have two secrets to keep."

Hunter watched Sue as she kept the smile plastered to her face long enough for Ned to get sucked into the lobby.

Then she turned toward him and smacked her palm against her forehead. "Who's taking pictures of me at my meetings?"

"The Falcon?"

"And then sending them to the CIA? For what earthly reason?"

"Sue…" Hunter took both of her hands. "The Falcon is gone…disappeared. Maybe his information was also compromised. Maybe someone else has those pictures and then fed them to the CIA to discredit you."

"Discredit?" She disentangled her hands from his and raked her fingers through her hair. "Those pictures can send me to federal prison. Of course, I didn't document those meetings. They were secret.

The Falcon always assured me that he had everything covered—even in the case of an emergency."

"Like this one?"

"Exactly." Sue grabbed her purse and smacked down the lid of his laptop. "Let's get going."

He smoothed his hand over his computer. "If you insist. Where?"

"We're going to talk to the one person who just might know what happened to The Falcon."

HUNTER WHEELED HIS rental car into the hospital parking lot, climbing up to the top floor of the structure. He cut the engine and folded his arms. "Are you sure you know what you're doing?"

Sue had already popped open her door and cranked her head over her shoulder. "We need to get in there and talk to this woman. She knew the code. She knows The Falcon. And she knew where to find me. She probably knows where The Falcon is, too. She's the only hope I have right now...or you can forget about helping Denver. If I'm locked up, you're never going to discover the link."

"I will leave it to your covert ops hands to get us into that hospital room when the nurse wouldn't even tell you if the woman regained consciousness." He yanked the keys from the ignition and opened his own door. "What if she hasn't?"

Sue slid out of the car and ducked her head back inside. "We'll have to come back."

Sue strode into the hospital like she owned the joint. Might as well come in with confidence.

They reached the elevator and she scanned the directory for the correct floor.

Hunter leaned over, touching his head to hers. "Do you know where you're going?"

"When the operator transferred me this morning, the nurse answered with the department—and this is it." She poked at the glass directory with her fingertip and then jabbed the elevator call button. "I just hope this elevator doesn't dump us out in front of the nurses' station."

"If it does?"

"We don't get off on that floor. We'll ride it up to the next."

"Tell me you've done this before." Hunter followed her into the elevator and then held the door for a woman with a tearful, sniffling baby.

Sue nudged Hunter's shoe with her toe. "Something like it."

Hunter ignored her in favor of wiggling his fingers at the baby, who gave him a watery smile and kicked his legs against his mommy's hip.

Sue pressed a hand against her belly. Hunter had wanted children with his ex, but she put him off and then dropped the bombshell that she didn't want kids at all.

When the elevator settled on the woman's floor, she nodded to Hunter. "Thanks for entertaining him right out of his fussiness. You must be a dad."

"Nah, babies just think I'm funny." He touched his finger to his nose and then the baby's. "Must be my nose."

When the doors closed, Sue cleared her throat. "When the doors open on our floor, if you see the nurses' station, press the button for the next floor up and we'll circle back down via the stairwell."

Hunter saluted. "Got it, chief."

"Don't get smart." She elbowed him in the ribs just as the doors whisked open on a short corridor, not a nurse in sight. "We're good."

Sue stepped from the elevator with Hunter close behind her and made a sharp right turn. Seconds later, she tugged on his sleeve and tipped her head toward a door marked Maintenance.

Hunter eased open the door and they both slipped inside the dark room, cluttered with cleaning supplies—and coveralls.

"This is you." She tugged a blue coverall from a hook and tossed it to him. "Slip into that and grab a mop."

"You're kidding."

"I'm not. Do you think the hospital staff knows the entire custodial staff or keeps track of the turnover?"

"What are you dressing up as for Halloween?"

"I'm going to try to snag myself a lab coat." She pinched his cheek. "This will work."

She cracked open the door and put her eye to the space, checking the hallway. She scooted out and checked on the offices and rooms on the corridor before heading upstairs. She had more luck on the research floor where there were no patients.

She lifted a lab coat from a hook just inside a

lounge area and stuck her arms into the sleeves. She jogged back downstairs and had even more luck on the way back to the custodians' closet when she ducked into an examination room and swiped a stethoscope from a silver tray.

As she continued down the corridor, she hung it around her neck and then dipped into the maintenance room.

She almost bumped into Hunter, the blue of his coveralls matching his eyes, holding a mop in one hand and a clipboard in the other.

"Hello, doc." He held out the clipboard to her. "Look what I found."

"See, you're catching on. I'll put in a good word for you at the Agency when you get cashiered out of Delta Force."

He leaned on his mop. "You're assuming *you're* going to have a job."

Turning the doorknob, she bumped the door with her hip. She held her breath as two nurses walked by.

She stepped into the hallway and whispered over her shoulder, "Give me a few minutes to find her room. I'll wait in front of her door and you can follow me inside."

Sue tucked her hair behind one ear and peered down at the clipboard in her hand that contained a cleaning rotation schedule instead of someone's vitals—but nobody had to know that.

It took her two passes down the stretch of hall with patient rooms before she located the double room the mystery woman occupied with another patient.

Hunter turned the corner, pushing the mop in front of him. Their eyes met for a split second before Sue crept into the room.

An African American woman hooked up to monitors and devices snored slightly from the first bed.

Sue jumped when the door creaked, and Hunter held his finger to his lips.

Sue said, "Our patient is in the next bed on the other side of the screen."

"Lucky for us, she's out of view of the door. If anyone comes in while we're here, you called me in for a cleanup."

"Got it." Sue tiptoed past the first bed and around the screen. She grabbed onto the footrest of the other bed where the woman from last night breathed through tubes.

"She looks worse than the other woman." Sue sidled up next to the bed. "Hello, it's me. It's Nightingale. Where's The Falcon? What do you know?"

The woman's eyelids flew open, and Sue jumped backward, gasping and dropping her clipboard.

"What happened?" Hunter materialized by her side, mop in hand.

Sue touched the woman's cool, papery arm. "She's awake."

"She can't talk, Sue." Hunter pointed to the mask over the woman's face.

"She's all I have right now, Hunter." She squeezed the woman's arm. "What can you tell me? You came to our hotel room, and you recited the code. Who are you? Where's The Falcon?"

The woman managed to roll her arm over and blink her eyes once.

"I don't know what you mean. Do you think you can write something?"

"Sue, she can't write. She can't grip a pen."

The woman turned her arm again and blinked.

"She can move her arm." Sue stroked the woman's flesh. "I'm sorry. I don't know what you mean. Maybe you can communicate to the nurses that you want to see me and when you're able to talk I'll come back."

The woman blinked her eyes twice and rolled her arm over again.

"She keeps moving her right arm."

"Maybe it's the only thing she can move right now."

The woman blinked without moving her arm this time and Sue glanced down. "Wait, Hunter."

"What?"

"She has something on her arm." Sue turned the woman's arm, so that her palm was displayed, and squinted at the tattoo on the inside of the woman's elbow.

She skimmed her thumb across the dark blue falcon imprinted on the woman's skin, then raised her gaze to meet the woman's glittering eyes above her mask.

"She's The Falcon."

Chapter Eleven

Before Hunter could respond to this news, the machines keeping The Falcon alive began to beep and whir.

"We'd better get out of here."

He grabbed Sue's hand and tugged, but she seemed rooted to the floor, her mouth working as she mumbled.

"A woman. I can't believe you're a woman." Sue grabbed a handful of white sheet. "Why? Why would you do that to another woman?"

He had no idea what Sue was rambling about, but they had to get out of here. He yanked on her lab coat. "Let's go."

Swinging around, he claimed his mop and pushed it in front of him out the door, almost colliding with three nurses in the corridor on their way to the distressed patient.

He cranked his head over his shoulder and let out a breath as he saw Sue following him. Without waiting for her, he careened around the corner and dumped his disguise in the maintenance room.

He made his way to the elevator, where he found Sue, head tilted back, watching the lights above the car as it descended, the lab coat still over her clothes.

They stepped into the elevator with several other people and continued to pretend they didn't know each other—not that it would've mattered to these strangers.

When they hit the parking structure, Hunter slowed down to let Sue catch up with him. Her white face and huge, glassy eyes caused his heart to bump in his chest.

He took her hand on the way to the car. "Are you sure she's The Falcon?"

"Positive." She chewed her bottom lip. "Didn't you see her tattoo?"

"Maybe she just got that to mark herself as someone in The Falcon's unit."

Sue turned on him and thrust out her arm, wrist turned outward. "Do you see one of those on me? That was not required—other things were required, but not that."

When they reached the car, Hunter opened the door for her but blocked her entrance into the car. "What's wrong, Sue? Why are you so shocked The Falcon is a woman? You yourself know women in the CIA can be as good as any man."

Her lashes fluttered. "I—I just never pictured The Falcon as a woman. I'm shocked…and I'm shocked that she showed up at my hotel room beaten and bloodied. How did that even happen? She's always worked behind the scenes—giving orders, issuing ultimatums."

Hunter stepped aside and Sue dropped to the car seat, covering her face with her hands.

He closed the door and shook his head on his way to the driver's side. It must be disconcerting to discover someone you assumed was one gender was another. He didn't get the big deal, but maybe it was a female thing—and he'd never voice *that* to Sue.

He slid behind the wheel and smoothed a lock of hair back from Sue's forehead. "At least The Falcon is still alive."

"As far as we know." She peeled her hands from her face. "She looked bad, and what happened at the end? That didn't sound good."

"How'd you get out of the room with all those nurses rushing in? Sorry I left you, but I figured it would look even weirder for a doctor and a maintenance guy to be in a patient's room while those bells and whistles were going off."

"That's okay. I would've expected you to get out while you could." She powered down the window and took a deep breath. "When I heard them coming, I waited until they were in the room, and then I stepped behind the screen. They never saw me."

"Thank God for that. I wouldn't want to see you accused of tampering with a patient on top of everything else you're going through."

Sue clasped her hands in her lap. "I think my very survival depends on finding a link between the terrorists The Falcon and I have been tracking and the ones Denver was onto. If I can uncover a terrorist plot here in the states, the CIA will have to believe I was working deep undercover—whether or not The Falcon survives."

"Maybe she'll out herself now and the whole operation before she takes a turn for the worse."

"Before she takes a turn for the worse?" Sue flung out her hands. "What were all those beeps and hisses from her machines? That sounded like a turn for the worse to me."

"The nurses were in there in a split second."

"If The Falcon dies..." Sue ended on a sob and covered her eyes with one hand.

"I know she's been someone important in your life, a mentor. Even if you hadn't met her, I'm sure it was hard to see her like that." Hunter rubbed his knuckles on the denim covering her thigh. "Now maybe you can understand what I'm going through with Denver in the crosshairs."

Sue's voice hardened along with her jaw. "The Falcon can rot in hell for all I care. She'd just better not take me down with her—again."

Hunter snatched his hand back and jerked his head to the side. "Whoa. Do you blame her for getting compromised? For comprising your position?"

"I blame her for a lot of things, Hunter." Sue dragged her thumb across her jaw. "And to think, all this time The Falcon was a female—a coldhearted, cold-blooded one."

Hunter braced his hands against the steering wheel and hunched his shoulders. "Why does it matter to you so much that The Falcon is a woman? Professional jealousy?"

He bit his tongue, literally. Did he just say that out loud?

Sue snorted, the nostrils of her longish nose flaring. "Yeah, that's it. Professional jealousy because I aspire to be a cold fish just like The Falcon...or is that a cold bird?"

Hunter gave up on the conversation and concentrated on the road. He didn't want to open his mouth again and blurt out the wrong thing, and Sue wasn't making much sense, anyway.

She descended deep in thought for the rest of the ride back to the hotel, her chin dropped to her chest.

At least she seemed more on board with his agenda, which seemed to have taken second place to all the drama swirling around Sue. But he'd lay odds that her drama was Denver's drama.

By the time they reached the hotel, Sue had climbed out of her funk—mostly.

"Pazir, huh?"

"What?" He pulled the car up to the valet stand.

"Denver's contact is Pazir, some Afghani who's working both sides over there?"

"That's right. Sound familiar now?"

"Not yet, but by the time I'm finished researching him, he's gonna be my best friend in the world." She shrugged out of the lab coat and tossed it in the back seat.

Back in the hotel room, Sue made a beeline for her laptop. "I have most of my files on here. It's secure. Email is encrypted. And my password is my fingerprint."

"All the latest and greatest stuff, but can you get to everything you need?"

"I can, but if your CIA buddy who likes to leave you gifts in mailboxes wants to play, I might need his help."

"I can get him on board. He knows Rex, and he wants to help."

"Rex?"

"Denver."

As Sue attacked her keyboard, Hunter crossed his arms and studied her from across the room. The Falcon's identity seemed to energize her, fueled by her puzzling resentment that The Falcon was a woman.

Sue raised her eyes from her laptop. "What? Why are you staring at me? Shouldn't you be on the phone to your CIA contact to see if he wants to play ball?"

"When we met in Paris, you said you were on assignment, although I didn't know it at the time."

"That's right." She planted her elbows on either side of her laptop, joined her hands and rested her chin on them. "So?"

"I'm not trying to grasp at straws here—or maybe I am—but is that why you had to leave me without a word, without a backward glance, without warning?"

"Technically, I left you word. I put a note on your pillow."

"Cut it. You know what I mean." He wedged a shoulder against the window, wondering again what they were doing in this hotel room instead of Sue's townhouse in Georgetown.

She closed her eyes for a second. "Yes, that's why. Do you think I wanted to leave you? Did last night feel like I wanted to leave you all those years ago?"

His jaw tightened. "The Falcon made you leave me. She's the one who told you never to contact me again."

"Bingo." Sue stared off into space. "I'd already been warned not to get personal with anyone while on a mission, but—" she shifted her gaze to him "—we couldn't help ourselves, could we?"

Warmth flooded his veins, washing away all the doubt and regret that had dogged him since his affair with Sue. After his divorce and his abandonment by Sue, he'd felt toxic.

His shoulders slumped and he sagged against the window.

Sue jumped up from her chair and flew toward him. Wrapping her arms around his waist, she choked, "I never wanted to leave you, Hunter. Never wanted to give up on you, on us, b-but my job depended on it. Maybe even my life."

He rested his cheek on top of her head. "And people think the military demands blind allegiance. Was the job important enough for you to give up…love?"

"I didn't know it was love." She pulled back from him and cupped his jaw with her hand. "Not then. We had a crazy chemical attraction for each other. When we weren't making love, we were talking to all hours of the morning, strolling along the Seine. It was like a magical dream, wasn't it?"

"It wasn't a dream. It was real." He thumped his chest with his fist. "I knew it then. Knew we had something special. The setting, the circumstances might have supercharged what we were feeling, but there was no denying what we were feeling."

"You'd just gotten out of a marriage. I knew it had been hard on you." She brushed her thumb over his lips. "I thought maybe I was just a rebound for you, someone to hold on to and make you feel again."

He raked a hand through his dark hair. "I can understand that. I can even understand slipping away when ordered to by The Falcon, but I can't understand the rest."

Her body stiffened. "The rest?"

"Never calling me, never reaching out." He snapped his fingers. "All it would've taken was one phone call. I would've followed you anywhere. Surely, even The Falcon realizes that CIA agents have relationships, marriages."

Sue broke away from him and stepped back. "I'm more than an agent. You know that now."

"So, once you join a black ops organization, you give up your personal life? I find that hard to believe." He flattened his hands against the cool window behind him.

She pressed the heel of her hand against her forehead. "You might find it hard to believe, but you see how I live—racing from one thing to another, always living on the edge, never knowing whom to trust."

"You're giving up on marriage, kids…love?" He reached out and captured a lock of her hair, slowly twisting it around his finger. "You're made for love, Sue. I see it."

Her cell phone buzzed on the table behind her, and she shifted her gaze to the side as he tightened his hold on her hair.

She jerked her thumb over her shoulder. "That might be important."

Expelling a long breath, he released his hold on her, maybe forever. Her priorities lay elsewhere and he couldn't change that.

She lunged for the phone. "It's the hospital. I'll put it on speaker."

Cradling the phone in her hand, she tapped the display and returned to him by the window, but their connection had been broken. She'd broken it.

"Hello?"

"Is this Sue Chandler?"

"It is."

"I'm calling about the injured woman who came to your hotel room last night."

"Yes?" Sue grabbed his arm.

"She's conscious and she's asking for you. Do you know who she is? She won't tell us her name, she had no ID on her and we can't fingerprint her without her consent. We're going to have to get the police involved, as she was a crime victim."

"I don't know who she is, but I'm curious to find out why she came to my room and why she wants to see me now. Maybe it's just to thank me, but could you hold off on calling the police until I talk to her? Maybe I can discover who she is."

"She just came to in the past few hours after a turn for the worse. She's still not out of the woods, so we have no intention of calling the police yet."

"Okay, I'll be there within the hour. Tell her I'll be there."

"Thank you."

Sue ended the call and then backed up, falling across the bed. "Thank God she's awake and okay."

"It doesn't sound like she's okay. The nurse said she's still in bad shape, but at least she's asking to see you." He sat on the edge of the bed. "I hope she plans to tell you how she was compromised and can set things right with the Agency."

"I hope she can tell me a lot of things."

They made the drive back to the hospital—a little faster this time and with more confidence. At least he had more confidence. Sue had never had any doubts they could get into The Falcon's hospital room.

This time they checked in at the nurses' station and were given the room number, which they pretended they didn't already know.

The same patient, hooked up to the same machines, in the same position greeted them when they entered The Falcon's hospital room.

Hunter hung back as Sue poked her head around the screen and said, "Are you awake?"

When Hunter heard a slight intake of breath, he

followed Sue around the screen. The Falcon didn't look much like a falcon.

The beating had taken a toll on the older woman in the bed. Two dark, penetrating eyes stared out from a worn face, crisscrossed with life's miseries and triumphs.

She rasped out one word. "Nightingale."

She could barely get out that name as it cracked on her lips, and Hunter's high hopes took a nosedive. How much could Sue get out of The Falcon in this condition? The woman looked as if she were on death's doorstep.

Sue dragged a chair over and sank into it while she took the older woman's hand. "What happened? How'd they get to you?"

The Falcon pointed a clawlike hand at the plastic water cup on the bedside table, and Hunter retrieved it for her and held the straw to her lips.

She drank and then waved him away. "Ambush."

"They ambushed you? How did they find you? The CIA doesn't even know who you are. I didn't even realize you were here in DC."

The Falcon coughed. "Whole mission over."

"No." Sue scooted her chair closer. "I don't believe that. I can't accept it. I gave up...everything for this mission."

The Falcon's gaze darted to Hunter and pierced him to his soul. She coughed again, and the beeping on her machines picked up speed. "Over. Too dangerous."

"Tell me what to do. I'll finish it." Sue reached for the water cup again as The Falcon went into another coughing fit.

"Over, Nightingale. Someone inside."

Hunter hunched forward. "Are you telling us there's someone on the inside of our own government working with terrorists against US interests?"

The Falcon placed her thin lips on the straw. When Sue pulled it away, a few drops of water dribbled from the corner of The Falcon's mouth.

"Deep. Someone deep. Major Rex Denver."

"No!" Hunter shouted the word. "He's not involved."

The Falcon reached out, and with unexpected strength, she wrapped her bony fingers around his wrist like a vise. "Someone inside setting up Denver. My shoe, Nightingale."

Sue's eyebrows arched. "Your shoe? What are you talking about? This isn't over, Falcon. I'm gonna see this through."

"Danger. Stop."

"There's always been danger. I'm not stopping now." Sue jumped from the plastic chair and it tipped over. "Why did you do it? Why did you ruin my life if you're going to give up so easily?"

"Necessary."

"Necessary but now it's over?"

Hunter drew his brows over his nose. How did The Falcon ruin Sue's life? If she was talking about their relationship, that wasn't over—and he had no intention of allowing Sue to end it now, black ops or no black ops.

"Had to do it, Nightingale. For the best."

"The best? Really? The best that I gave up the man I loved and our...son?"

Chapter Twelve

A sudden fog descended on Hunter's brain activity. What the hell was Sue talking about? Son? She didn't have a son. They didn't have a son.

Another coughing fit seized The Falcon, and her face turned blue while the machines went crazy.

This time the nurses arrived even faster, and as they swarmed the room and clustered around the bed, Hunter tugged on Sue's arm.

"Her shoe. Get The Falcon's shoe."

Sue turned a blank face toward him as one tear seeped from the corner of her eye.

He dived past her and yanked open the door of a cabinet. He plunged his hand into the folded stack of The Falcon's bloodstained clothes, and his fingers curled around a pair of sneakers. He clasped them to his chest, unnoticed by the nurses and by Sue herself, still rooted to the floor, in a daze watching the medical efforts to save The Falcon's life.

Hunter grabbed her hand and pulled her out of the room, past a doctor rushing in to take their place.

He propelled Sue to the elevator and out to the

car, where he tossed The Falcon's shoes in the back seat. He'd deal with those later. There was so much more to deal with in the seat next to him.

His throat tight, he closed his eyes and he took a deep breath. "Sue, what was all that about our son?"

She slumped in her seat and clasped her hands between her knees. "It's true. I'm sorry, Hunter. I got pregnant in Paris and had a son. Drake is almost three."

Her words punched him in the gut and for several seconds he couldn't breathe. For the second time in his life a woman had lied to him about children—but this was much worse than his ex changing her mind about having them. He'd had a son out there for three years and never knew.

A wave of rage overwhelmed him and he punched the dashboard, leaving a crack—like he felt in his heart right now. "Why?"

"Do I have to tell you that after what you just heard?"

He rubbed his knuckles. "You kept my son from me because The Falcon told you to?"

"Yes. I had to. I had to comply."

"Your job was more important...is more important, than anything else in your life?" He snorted. "What a sad life you lead."

Sue sniffed and the tears she seemed to be holding back spilled over and coursed down her cheeks. "You don't think I know that?"

"Where is he now? Where's...Drake?" The unfamiliar name stuck on his tongue and the rage burned in his gut again.

"He's with my dad and my stepmom."

Hunter whistled through his teeth. "That's great. He's with a woman who detests you and a father who groomed you for a soulless, empty career with the CIA. Don't tell me. It was your father's idea for you to go black ops. His little girl fulfilling everything he hadn't in his career."

Sue pressed her fingers against her temples. "Drake lives with my sister, Amelia, and her family in South Carolina. They went to the Bahamas and I didn't want Drake to go, so he spent some time with me first and then I sent him with my parents."

"Our son doesn't even live with his mother." Hunter bowed his head and rested his forehead against the steering wheel. How did this happen?

He felt Sue's hand on the back of his neck, and he stiffened, his first instinct to shrug her off—this woman who'd tricked him and lied to him at every turn.

But her touch turned to a caress as she stroked his flesh with her fingers. "I'm sorry, Hunter. I thought it was best for Drake to live with my sister while I'm involved in all this. Can you imagine if he lived with me and I failed to return home one night? Or worse, what if I were home with him and someone broke in with a weapon, like how someone stormed our hotel room the other night?"

"Why even have him if you weren't going to keep him?"

Her hand trailed down his back. "There was never any question that I'd have your baby, regardless of how I chose to care for him later. I was thrilled with my pregnancy and never thought about my situation until...I told The Falcon."

He lifted his head. "She's the one who told you to send Drake away."

"Yes."

"Is she the one who told you not to tell me about the baby?" He tried to swallow the bitterness filling his mouth.

"Ordered me. She ordered me to keep quiet and explained the difficulties of raising a child for someone in my position."

"And then she sent you off to Istanbul and Berlin and God knows where else to make the point, right?" He cranked on the car engine, and Sue went back to her own side of the car.

"Do you think she kept me busy on purpose?" She dragged her hands across her face and peered at him through her fingers.

"She must've had a lonely, desolate life herself. She wanted to make sure you had the same." He pulled out of the parking garage so fast the car jumped and Sue grabbed the edge of her seat. "Isn't that why you were so angry when you found out The Falcon was a woman? You could understand a *man* telling you to give up your child, keep him from his father, be a part-time mother. But coming from a *woman*? That must've felt like betrayal."

Sue crossed her arms. "I guess so."

"I'm taking us back to the hotel, or do we even need the pretense now? You did keep me away from your townhouse because there's evidence of Drake all over that place, isn't there?"

"There is and I did." She dropped her chin to her chest. "But that's not the only reason. I really did believe we were safer at the hotel."

"Do you want me to take you home now? Forget this whole thing? Go back to your life?"

She whipped her head around. "Go back to my life? This *is* my life now. Like I told The Falcon, I have sacrificed too much to walk away now. I can't walk away, anyway. I'm under suspension and suspicion at the Agency, and I'm going to be cleared there only when The Falcon speaks up. Besides, didn't you hear The Falcon? There's someone on the inside and that someone is responsible for setting up Major Denver and probably for outing The Falcon's operation."

He nodded and squeezed the steering wheel. "I want to see my son, Sue. I want to meet Drake."

"You will." She traced the corded muscle on his forearm. "Can we wait until this is all over? We can go down to South Carolina together. He's just starting to ask about his father, and I can't wait to introduce him."

"I could've taken him, you know. I could've taken care of him."

"Hunter, you're in the army still getting deployed."

She was right, but he'd be damned if he were going to admit anything. He pulled in front of the hotel and said with a grimace on his lips, "Home sweet home."

She pointed into the back seat. "Don't forget the shoes. Why did you take her shoes?"

"Didn't you hear her? She mentioned her shoes. She distinctly said something about her shoes when half of what she said wasn't distinct at all, but that I caught."

"I'm glad you grabbed them. I was just so consumed by my anger at the time."

"I know how you feel."

They landed in the console, and Hunter picked up one of the small size sixes and shoved his hand inside. He peeled back the insole and ran his finger around the edge of the shoe.

Sue's phone buzzed in the cup holder, and as she picked it up, Hunter picked up the other shoe and repeated the process. "Go ahead."

She glanced at her phone's display. "It's the hospital."

As she spoke in monosyllables, Hunter removed the insole of the second shoe. He peeled up a small piece of paper stuck to the bottom inside of the shoe and unfolded it.

He whispered, "This is it, Sue—The Falcon left an address and a code."

She ended the call and cupped her phone between her hands. "That's good...because The Falcon is dead."

Chapter Thirteen

Sue dropped the phone in her lap and tilted back her head. "Can this day get any worse?"

"I'm sorry." Hunter touched her hand.

He must still be under the impression that The Falcon represented some feminist mentor to her or something, when all she'd felt for the frail woman in the hospital bed was contempt and anger. And now the woman had failed her again.

"How am I going to prove anything to the Agency without The Falcon? I have no idea what umbrella she was under or where she was getting her orders."

Hunter held up a shiny piece of paper pinched between his fingers. "I told you. There's an address and a code on this piece of paper. It was hidden beneath the insole of her shoe. She told you to get her shoes, and this is why."

"An address to what? A code for what?" Sue scooped her hair back from her face. "She left me flapping in the breeze. I'll have no explanation for the investigators when they ask me about those photo ops with terrorists—unsanctioned."

"We'll get there, Sue, and we're gonna start with this slip of paper."

Hunter's blue eyes bored into her, shoring her up, giving her strength. And she'd just rocked the foundation of his world.

"Okay, I'll try to have as much faith in that info as you do." She squared her shoulders. "I'm sorry I didn't tell you about Drake. It was cruel and wrong."

"You were just…" He pocketed the precious piece of paper. "Hell, I don't know what you were doing. You've told me so many lies, I don't know what to believe about you, Sue."

"Just believe I have regrets, and we'll leave it at that for now." She pointed out the window. "The valet has been champing at the bit to park your car and get it out of the way."

"Then let's give him that opportunity. We'll regroup, get lunch and find this address." He patted his front pocket.

Back in the hotel room, Hunter entered The Falcon's address on his laptop. He smacked the table. "It's a storage unit in Virginia. There could be a treasure trove of information in there."

"Why would she keep hard copies?"

"Laptops—" he pinged the side of his "—can get stolen."

"Even if my laptop disappeared, whoever took it would have a hard time accessing any data on it. We have so many layers of security on our stuff."

"Really? Because I'm pretty sure someone used

that hacking group, Dreadworm, to access CIA emails to get the ball rolling against Major Denver."

"Maybe, maybe not." She reached into the mini-fridge and snagged a bottle of water. "If what The Falcon said is true, there's someone on the inside pulling the strings for this terrorist group. He…or she could easily cover his…or her tracks."

Hunter snapped his laptop shut. "Are you ready to head over there now, or do you want to stop and get something to eat?"

"I don't think the storage unit is going anywhere and you look like you could use some food—and some pictures."

"Pictures?"

"Of Drake." She grabbed her purse. "Let's go back to my place before we eat. I have to collect my mail and water a few plants."

"I was going to ask before, but I figured you might not want to carry any pictures of him." Hunter slipped his laptop into its sleeve and tucked it under his arm. "You don't have any pictures on your phone?"

"I don't keep pictures of Drake on my phone— just in case."

"The Agency must know you have a child. You can't keep that kind of information a secret from your employer—especially a government employer like the CIA."

"My employer knows. The pregnancy and birth were covered by my insurance, of course, but I took a leave of absence for five months. None of my coworkers know I have a child. They know I'm close to my nieces and...nephew, but that's it."

"That's crazy, Sue." He rested one hand on her shoulder. "You know that, right?"

"I know, but it makes sense—or made sense for me."

"And it was something The Falcon suggested."

"Working a black ops team is special, Hunter, different. We follow different rules, live different lives." She folded her arms over her purse, pressing it to her stomach. "I'll bet you Major Denver isn't married, is he? No children? No long-term relationships for him. He's not only your Delta Force commander. Someone is using him for intel. He's no different from me."

Hunter blinked his thick, black lashes. "Major Denver's wife and child were killed by a drunk driver. It gutted him. He changed after that, became harder, fiercer and more determined."

"A man with nothing to lose."

"That's right, but you..."

"My mother died from an aggressive form of breast cancer at a particularly vulnerable time in my life. I suffered from depression. I even made a half-hearted attempt to commit suicide, but my father rescued me."

"I had no idea." He touched her cheek. "I'm sorry. How did your father help?"

"I had already shown an aptitude for languages, so he encouraged me, sent me to boarding school in Switzerland for a few years, where I picked up more languages...and a purpose in my life." She lifted her shoulders. "So, your interpretation of my father's grooming me to fulfill his CIA dreams may be true, but it saved my life."

His mouth lifted on one side. "I don't know what the hell I was talking about. I just wanted to strike out at you."

"Understandable and deserved." She took his hand and kissed the rough palm. "Now, let me show you those pictures."

As they got into the car, he leaned over and tapped the phone in her hand. "You haven't looked at the barbershop video in a while. You said Jeffrey admitted we landed on their radar the minute we walked into that barbershop. That means you did have the right barbershop all along. Are you ready now to tell me how you heard about the shop and Walid?"

"Drive." She snatched his phone and entered her address in the GPS, although he probably already had it in there. "When my terrorist contacts pretended to kidnap me in Istanbul, they did so in order for me to pass them information about a raid, which of course was completely made up. The most valuable time I spend with my contacts is when they speak among each other in their own language. They have no idea I know their language, and it's the best way for me to pick up information."

"No wonder The Falcon wanted to keep you on her team by any means necessary. Go on."

"There I was, drinking tea and rubbing a rope against my wrists to prove I'd been held captive instead of turning over intelligence—even if it was fake intelligence." She smoothed a finger over her skin, which had long since healed but looked raw enough after her so-called escape. "They weren't paying much attention to me. They'd already paid me off."

"They thought you were doing it for the money?"

"Oh, yeah. The Falcon had manufactured some gambling debts for me...and several illegal prescriptions for drugs."

"Sue—" the steering wheel jerked in his hands "—would the CIA internal investigators see those things, also?"

"I'm pretty sure they would." She held up one hand. "I know. Don't say it. I already know I'm in big trouble if The Falcon's storage unit doesn't yield any proof of our deep undercover operation."

"I didn't mean to interrupt. Go on. They were ignoring you and talking among themselves without a clue that you could understand everything they were saying."

"That's right. And what they were saying had something to do with picking up materials from a barber named Walid at the shop on that corner. Like a dutiful little spy, I passed that info along to The Falcon. Two days ago, she called me and said the information was false and that there was no Walid at the shop."

"How did she know that?"

Sue spread her palms in front of her. "I was not privy to that sort of information. The Falcon told me it was the wrong barbershop."

"Maybe that's how they made The Falcon…and you. It was some kind of trap. They became aware somehow that you knew their language and they set you up, just like you'd been setting them up with your fake intel."

"Maybe you're right, but it's hard to believe The Falcon would expose herself like that. She was a pro." Sue pressed her fingers against her lips.

"What's wrong?"

"A pro. That's what she always used to call me. She knew she'd asked a lot of me—giving you up for good and then turning my son over to my sister. It was her ultimate compliment, but she was just playing me as surely as she played those terrorists."

"Nice neighborhood you have here." Hunter pointed out the window to the cherry trees lining her block, their pink blossoms preparing to explode with the next spring shower.

"But you've been here before." She tilted her head at him. "Why didn't you come up to my door that night? You'd come to DC specifically to contact me, right? Why skulk around and follow me to bars?"

He pulled up to the curb and put the car into Park. "The truth? I didn't know what I'd find when I got here—husband…children."

She coughed. "Little did you know."

"When you left me in that hotel room, I considered calling you anyway, even though you'd asked me not to contact you. I even looked you up once or twice."

"Let me guess—your CIA friend. Because my address and phone number are not easy to find."

"Don't be too hard on him. I never got your phone number, which is a good thing because it would've been less stressful to place a call or, better yet, leave a voice mail."

"What stopped you from looking me up in person?"

"Pride, I guess. I'd spent enough time trying to make things work with my wife. I didn't want to face any more rejection."

"I half expected you to show up on my doorstep one day."

"And you would've slammed that door in my face?"

"I would've thrown it open and fallen into your arms."

He snorted. "That's not exactly what you did when you woke up in my hotel room."

"Different circumstances." She tapped on the window. "You can't park here. You'll get a ticket. You can park behind my car in the garage."

She directed him around the corner to her parking spot. "You can block me in for now. I'm not going anywhere."

With her key chain dangling from her fingers, she led him through the garage to her back door, which faced an alley. She unlocked the door and pushed it open.

"No killer cats going to spring on me?"

"No, but Drake loves animals and I'm going to get

him a puppy…one day." She stepped into the kitchen and wrinkled her nose at the mess on the counter. "I didn't leave…"

Hunter wrapped an arm around her waist and dragged her backward into the alley, hissing in her ear, "Someone's in your place."

Sue arched her back. "I'm done with this. If they're in there, let's find out what they want."

Hunter cocked his head. "I don't hear any doors slamming or cars starting. Wait here and I'll check it out."

"Are you kidding?" She practically ripped the zipper from the outer pocket of her purse, which concealed her weapon.

"At least let me go in first."

She huffed out a breath, her nostrils flaring.

"Humor me." He withdrew his own gun and crept back into the kitchen with Sue's hot breath on his neck.

Leading with his weapon, he crossed the tile floor. The kitchen opened onto a small dining area, the round table adorned with a lacy tablecloth and a vase full of half-wilting flowers. He turned the corner and caught his breath.

Sue swore behind him at the upended drawers and bookshelves in disarray. Colorful pillows from the sofa dotted the floor.

"Looks like they didn't plan to keep their visit a secret."

"Shh." He nudged her shoulder as she drew up beside him.

"If they don't know we're here yet, they're too dumb to surprise us now." She waved her gun around the living room. "There's a half bathroom down here and then two bedrooms and a full bath upstairs."

Hunter glanced at a few photos of a child strewn across the floor, but he didn't have time to look yet.

As Sue placed a foot on the first step, he squeezed past her to take the lead. She'd done enough on her own these past three years. She had nothing to prove.

He made his way up the staircase, then checked both rooms, swallowing hard as he entered the room with the pint-size bed shaped like a car and the puppy-themed border of wallpaper ringing the room.

He checked out the closet, crammed with toys, and then backed out to join Sue in the bathroom, which had also been ransacked.

He wedged a foot on the edge of the tub, brushing aside the shower curtain dotted with red-and-blue fish. "What the hell were they looking for in here?"

"Maybe all my illegal meds."

Sue backed out of the bathroom and returned to her bedroom where she smoothed a hand over her floral bedspread. "Bastards. What do they think I have?"

Hunter crouched down beside the bed and stirred the shards of broken glass on a framed picture of a small boy hugging a rabbit. "He has black hair."

"And the bluest eyes ever—just like his dad." Sue

perched on the end of her bed. "This is not how I wanted you to see him."

"But then you never wanted me to see him, did you?"

Biting her lip, she rubbed the back of her hand across her stinging nose. Of course, Hunter wouldn't get over her deception as fast as his casual attitude made it seem he had. The resentment toward her burned deep inside him.

But working with her to clear Denver had to take precedence over any lashing out against her. He couldn't afford to alienate her now. He had to put his work first, too, maybe not to the degree that she'd put hers, but he had to understand what had been at stake for her.

She'd disobeyed direct orders by having a fling in Paris while she was on assignment—and a fling with a military man had just made the infraction worse. She'd doubled down with the pregnancy and her decision to keep the baby—as if she could've come to any other.

When The Falcon had told her to forget Hunter and keep her baby a secret, she'd finally complied—but what a price she'd paid.

She sighed. "Do you want to help me clean up?"

Cranking his head from side to side, he asked, "Is anything missing?"

"Anything of importance? No. I have my laptop with me, my phones. Anything else?" She shrugged. "Don't care. They didn't come here to rob me, did they?"

He straightened up with the frame in his hand. "Do you have a trash bag for this glass?"

"I'll grab some." When she returned upstairs with two plastic garbage bags, Hunter had another photo of Drake in his hands.

"He looks like a happy boy."

"Amelia and Ben live on Shelter Island off the coast of South Carolina. Drake loves it there, loves his two cousins, loves the beach." Her voice hitched. Did she have to tell Hunter that sometimes Drake cried for his mommy in the middle of the night or that he'd started saying the word *daddy* with alarming frequency? Time enough for that.

"But he'd rather be home with his mother?"

"Here." She shoved a plastic bag at him. "You can dump that glass in here. I'll take care of my clothes."

As Sue yanked open her drawers and folded and replaced the clothing that had been tossed, Hunter walked around the room straightening the furniture and picking up books, pictures and knickknacks.

Once her bedroom had been put together again, they moved on to Drake's room. The intruders hadn't spared her son's belongings. Whatever they suspected her of hiding, they'd figured that among kids' toys might just be the perfect spot.

This room took longer to set right as Hunter spent much of his time examining Drake's toys and testing them out. Finally, she trailed downstairs and got to work on the living room.

As Hunter picked up pillows and tossed them back onto the couch, she organized her shelves. Had they been sending her a message by having a total disregard for her possessions? Breaking items? Scattering things across the floor?

She stooped to pick up a frame lying facedown on the floor. The picture had slipped out, but she knew what had been in here.

Sue dropped to her hands and knees and scoured the floor, checking beneath the coffee table.

Hunter tousled her hair as he walked by. "I'll start tackling the kitchen."

Sue passed her hand beneath the sofa and then sat back on her heels, her heart fluttering in her chest. "You know how I told you upstairs I didn't think anything of importance was missing?"

"Yeah." Hunter stopped at the entrance to the dining area, his hand braced against the wall.

"I was wrong."

"What's missing?"

"They took a picture of Drake."

Chapter Fourteen

Hunter tripped to a stop as a shot of adrenaline spiked through his system. "You're sure? Did you check under the sofa?"

She held up an empty picture frame. "It was in here—a shot of him at the beach just a few months ago. It was my most recent picture of him."

When Hunter thought his legs could function properly, he pushed off the wall and joined Sue on the floor. Shoulder to shoulder, they searched the floor for the missing picture.

He even pulled all the cushions off the sofa to check behind them. "We don't know if they took it on purpose or it was stuck to something else they took out of here, or maybe it's still lost in the house somewhere."

Sue remained on the floor, legs curled beneath her. "Why would they take a picture of Drake unless they wanted to know what he looked like?"

"They have no way of knowing where he is, right?" He stretched out a hand to Sue and helped her to her feet, pulling her into his arms.

He'd wanted to remain angry at her for keeping Drake from him and a core of that anger still burned in his gut, but she was the mother of his son. He had a son, and the joy of that reality blotted out every other negative feeling.

"You're going to call your parents ASAP and tell them to keep an extra eye on Drake. Your father, at least, will understand the significance of that, won't he?"

"I'll make him understand." She broke away from him and pounced on her purse, dragging her cell phone from an outside pocket.

"You make that call, and I'll work on the kitchen. Hell, I might even locate that picture. On the beach, right?"

She dipped her head, wide-eyed, and tapped her phone to place the call.

As Hunter banged pots and pans back into what he hoped were their right places, he strained to hear Sue from the next room, but all he got was worried murmurs. He hoped the old CIA man was up to the task.

When she joined him in the kitchen, her face had lost its sharp angles. "My dad's on it. I think it'll be fine. They live in a pretty small town, and it's not like Drake is even school-age and out of their sight."

"That sounds good." He swung open a cupboard door. "Is this right?"

They finished putting the house back together and Sue watered her plants and collected the mail that was at least in a locked mailbox in the front— not that the intruders couldn't have broken into the mailbox. They'd done a bang-up job of breaking into Sue's house and wreaking havoc without raising any suspicion in the neighborhood.

When they were back in the car, Sue turned to him as she snapped her seat belt. "Should we head straight to the storage unit and skip lunch?"

"Are you kidding?" He patted his stomach. "That breakfast seems like a long time ago."

"It was. It's still not daylight saving time and this lunch is more like dinner and it might be dark by the time we get to the storage unit."

"People check on their stuff at all hours of the day and night. I checked their website, and they're open twenty-four hours, as long as you have the code for the gate—and we have it."

"She wrote down two sets of numbers. Do you think one set is for a lock?"

"I hope so, because we don't have a key, and I don't feel like breaking into a storage unit. The company probably has those units under CCTV surveillance, and we wouldn't last long trying to break into her unit."

"Then lunch—or dinner it is. Luckily, the place I had in mind for lunch serves dinner, too, and it's not too fussy, so we can get a quick bite and head out to the units."

They did just that, and as Hunter shoveled the last forkful of mashed potatoes into his mouth, Sue waved down the waiter for their check.

She pulled out her wallet before he could even wipe his hands on his napkin. "I'll get this one."

Hunter dragged the napkin across his face. "You seem like you're in a big hurry now when before you acted like we had all the time in the world."

"Yeah, that was before those lowlifes broke into my place and trashed it, stole a picture of Drake." She waved the check and her credit card at the waiter.

Sensing her urgency, the waiter returned with the receipt in record time and Sue stood up and scribbled her signature. "It's still somewhat light out."

Hunter dragged his jacket from the back of the chair. "Why are you so hell-bent on getting to this storage place before dark?"

"Storage units are creepy enough without having a pack of terrorists dogging your every move."

"There's no way they know where this place is. That paper was hidden in The Falcon's shoe, and they didn't find it when they searched her."

"I don't know. They seem to be everywhere we are."

As she headed for the door, Hunter gulped down the last of his water and followed her out to the car. He'd already put the storage unit address into his phone's GPS, and he turned it on when they got into the car.

"Just forty minutes away."

Sue cranked her head over her shoulder. "I hope nobody followed us from my place."

"Did you notice anyone? You had your eyes on your mirror the whole way over here."

"I didn't, but then I didn't notice anyone following us from the barbershop, did you?"

"Wasn't looking." He adjusted his own rearview mirror and watched a white car pull out behind them. He eased out a breath when the car turned off. "Now you have me jumpy."

"Good." She punched his arm. "You should be."

"You know, we've been going a mile a minute since I found out I had a son. You were supposed to fill me in at your place, but we were otherwise engaged there, and then we spent our meal talking about The Falcon's storage facility." He drew a cross over his heart. "I promise—no recriminations. I know I don't need to repeat how disappointed I am or…upset."

"That sounds like recriminations to me." She set her jaw and turned her head to stare out the window.

"I'm sorry." He rolled his shoulders. "Did I also tell you how happy I am to have a child? I can't wait to meet him, and I want to play a role in his life—including financial. I'll pay child support or whatever the courts order."

"I hope we don't have to go that route. We can figure this out together without lawyers or courts, can't we?"

"I'd like that. Now tell me about Drake. Does he have a middle name?" His head jerked toward her. "What's his last name?"

"I-it's Chandler. I had to do that, but we can change it to Mancini. I don't have a problem with that."

She slid him a sideways glance, probably to see

if he planned to slam his fist into the dash again. He didn't. Drake Mancini.

"Middle name?"

"It's Hunter."

He swallowed the lump that had suddenly formed in his throat. "Thanks for that."

"It was the least I could do."

Then she launched into a history of Drake Hunter Mancini—his likes, his dislikes, his first everythings.

He raised one eyebrow at her. "Does he ask about a daddy?"

"He's practicing the word. Amelia's husband is his father figure—for now—but he calls him Uncle Ben, not Daddy." She twisted her fingers in her lap. "I always figured those questions would come once he started school and saw all the other dads. Now we can avoid that."

Too soon, he took the turnoff for the storage units, located in a light industrial area of Virginia. He'd already memorized the address and the two codes, and as they pulled up to the security gate, he leaned out the window and entered the first code The Falcon had written on that slip of paper.

The gate glided open, and Hunter turned to Sue to share a fist bump. "First hurdle."

Sue pressed her nose to the window glass. "This first row has units in the hundreds. Hers is in the five hundreds."

He rolled to the end of the first row. "Right or left?"

"There's a sign up ahead. Drive forward."

As the headlights illuminated the sign, they both said at the same time, "Left."

Hunter swung the car around the corner. "These are three hundreds and the numbers are getting bigger."

"They just jumped from three to five. This is our row."

Hunter slowed the car to a crawl as Sue called out the storage unit numbers until she recited The Falcon's.

He parked vertically in front of unit number 533, leaving on his headlights. "Just in case the unit doesn't have a light inside."

"Great. We're going to have to fumble around in there in the dark?"

"We'll see." Hunter scrambled from the car, the second code running through his head. He punched it in to the keypad, and the lock on the big silver sliding door clicked on the other side.

He grabbed the handle and yanked it to the side. The door opened with a squeal, and he rolled it wide.

Tipping his head back, he said, "Looks like there's no light source inside."

"Why are they open twenty-four hours if they don't provide lighting in the units?" Sue brushed past him to step inside the chilly space. "Or heating."

Hunter jerked his thumb over his shoulder. "I guess you have to provide your own. You have about twenty cell phones on you now, don't you? We can use all those flashlights."

She tapped the phone in her hand and a beam of

light shot out from it. "I have just my own phone right now, but yours and mine should be able to do the trick, and once you move out of the way, those headlights should at least let us see what's in here."

He shoved the door to the end and shifted to the side to allow the lights from the car to flood the unit.

Sue lifted her nose to the air. "At least she didn't stash any dead bodies in here."

"That doesn't mean there aren't a few skeletons in her unit...or her closet." He kicked the bottom box of a stack. "I hope these aren't files."

"One way to find out." Sue attacked the box on the top, lifting the lid and knocking it to the floor. She sneezed. "Kind of dusty."

He sidled up next to her, aiming the light from his phone into the box. "What's in here?"

Sue reached inside and pulled out three passports. She fanned them under the light. "Two US, one Canadian."

Hunter plucked one from her fingers and thumbed it open. "It's not The Falcon. It's a man. Recognize him?"

Sue rubbed her finger across the picture. "Nope."

Hunter flipped open the other two passports. They featured the same man, his appearance slightly altered with glasses, facial hair, different colored contacts...and a different name.

Sue dug through the rest of the box's contents. "Same stuff. Passports, some birth certificates— everything you need to establish a fake identity for purposes of travel."

"These must be all the agents The Falcon used for her black ops missions."

Sue rapped on the second box. "This proves she *did* have black ops missions, anyway, doesn't it? Helps me out."

"Let's keep looking for something more recent." Hunter kicked another box and crouched down to paw through some gadgets. "This is regular spy stuff here—old cameras, listening devices."

"Why would she want me to see all this stuff?" Sue hoisted the box on top and settled it on the floor. She replaced its lid and dived into the second box. "More of the same."

"It proves she was running an operation, for sure, or several operations."

Sue gasped. "Oh my God."

Hunter spun around. "What is it?"

"My father." She held up a passport in each hand and waved them. "These are my father's. He must've worked with or for The Falcon himself."

"Is there any doubt now he got you into the unit?"

She fired the passports back into the box. "He had to know the price I had to pay. He was allowed to have a family and a home life before opting into that unit."

"You're done with that now, Sue. The Falcon is dead. The mission is over. You need to get your life back."

She waved her arm at the stacks. "And all this is gonna help me. I need my job…and my reputation back."

Hunter tripped over a metal filing cabinet. He flipped it open and rifled through the contents. "This is more like it. Paperwork on some of her missions. Forget the passports and spy gadgets. This is the stuff we need."

Sue stepped over a stuffed suitcase and crouched before another filing cabinet. "At least this one doesn't have two inches of dust coating it."

"Yeah, those are the ones we need to be looking at. I'm sure she directed you to this storage unit for a reason—and it wasn't to find your father's fake passports."

"Okay, minimal dust." Sue's muffled voice came from the back of the unit.

Still in a crouch, Hunter moved two steps to the side and ducked into another filing cabinet. The headlights beaming into the unit flickered.

He called out to Sue. "I hope my car battery's not dying."

"That's all you need. You already cracked the dash."

The lights flickered again and Hunter twisted his head over his shoulder. A flash of light illuminated the space, blinding him.

An explosion rocked the unit and then the sliding door squealed closed—trapping them inside with the blaze.

Chapter Fifteen

The explosion had thrown Sue backward, and she clutched a stack of folders to her chest as she fell to the floor.

As the acrid smoke burned her eyes and lungs, she screamed for Hunter. He'd been behind her, closer to the source of the blast...and now the fire that raged, blocking their exit from the storage unit.

"Sue, are you all right?"

At the sound of Hunter's voice, she choked out a sob. "I'm here. I'm okay."

The boxes provided fuel for the flames and they licked greedily at their sustenance as they danced closer to the back of the unit. Sue flattened her body on the cement floor, the files digging into her belly.

Hunter appeared, crawling through the gray smoke. "Thank God you're not hurt. You're not, are you?"

"No. You?"

"Fine." He even scooted forward and kissed the tip of her nose. "Don't worry. I have a plan."

"The fire's blocking the door, isn't it?" She rubbed

her stinging eyes. "What kind of plan could you possibly have?"

"All those spy gadgets I was making fun of?" He reached behind him and dragged a box forward that looked as if it contained wet suits.

"We're trapped in a room with fire. We're not underwater." Her gaze shifted over his head and her nostrils flared. "It's bad, Hunter."

He pulled one of the wet suits from the box. "These aren't wet suits, Sue. They're fire-retardant suits. They'll allow us to literally walk through flames—if they're not too old and decrepit."

"Why'd you have to add that last part?" She snatched the suit from his hands and shimmied into it while she was on the ground.

"Pull up the hood and put on the gloves." A crash made her jump but Hunter didn't blink an eye. "Hurry! There's netting that drops over the face but cover your face with your gloved hands. Make sure your hair is all tucked in and hang on to me."

Suited up, they crawled across the floor for as long as they could. Then Hunter gave her the command to stand up in the fire.

Sue's mind went blank as she covered her face with one hand and kept the other pressed against Hunter's back. She had a moment of panic when they reached the door, but Hunter yanked it back.

As the air rushed into the storage unit, the flames surged, but Hunter dragged her outside. He pulled her several feet away from the blazing unit and then left her.

Seconds later, she heard the car idling beside her. As she lurched to her knees, Hunter came around behind her and hoisted her to her feet, half dragging, half carrying her to the car.

With her door still hanging open, Hunter punched the accelerator and they sped from the facility. Once outside, he pulled over beneath a freeway on-ramp. "Call 911 from your burner phone."

She reached for the phone on the console, but her thick gloves wouldn't allow her to pick it up.

"I've got it." Hunter yanked off one of his gloves and made the call to 911 to report the fire.

Then he flipped back his hood. "Are you all right? Did you get through okay?"

Sue pounded her chest through her suit. "I think so, but my lungs hurt."

"Mine too. Let's take these things off and see if they worked."

"We're sitting here talking to each other." She reached out and smoothed a thumb over one of his eyebrows. "Outside of some singed hair, I'd say we made it."

Hunter got out of the car and tugged at the suit, kicking it off his legs. He ran his hands over his arms, legs and head. He poked his head into the car. "Do you like that thing so much you plan to wear it?"

Sue hugged herself. "I love it. It saved our lives."

Hunter walked around to the passenger's side and opened the door. "I'll help you."

As she slid out of the car, sirens wailed in the distance. "At least the fire engines are on the way, but the cops are going to wonder why we left the scene. Your rental car is going to be on camera, along with our activities."

"Along with the activities of the people who tossed that explosive device into the unit?" Hunter ripped at the Velcro closure around her neck. "Do you really think they would allow that?"

"What do you mean? You think they disabled the security system?"

"I'm sure of it. They're professionals. There's no way they would be seen on camera—even disguised."

As she stepped out of the suit, Sue ran a hand through her tangled hair, which seemed to have a few crispy ends. "How'd you get that door open? I thought they'd slid it closed, trapping us inside."

"That door won't close without the code. They could slide it shut and maybe they even thought they were locking us in, but you need the code to do that."

"Thank God." She clung to him for a second to steady herself. "I—I thought we were going to die, although really my mind was numb. Looking back, I realize we could've died."

"That's the important thing...but I felt that we were getting so close to finding what we wanted. I suppose if everything's not burned to a crisp, we could try to get back in there."

"We might be okay."

"Yeah, I suppose if you can get us into the hospital room of Jane Doe patients, you can get us into burned-out storage units."

"No, I mean I think we might be okay." Sue pulled up her shirt and gripped the edge of the file folders stuffed into her pants.

Hunter took a step back. "What the hell?"

"You thought we were getting close—we were." She waved the file folders at him. "Do you know how these are labeled?"

"I'd have to get my phone to see. Don't be a tease."

She held the folders in front of her face and kissed the top one. "Denver Assignment."

Hunter wrapped his arms around her and swung her through the air. "I could kiss you."

"Do it."

He set her down and grabbed her face with his hands. He puckered up and pressed a kiss against her mouth that nearly swept her off her feet again.

Back in the car, she shuffled through The Falcon's notes. "Let's not get too excited. We need to find out how they tracked us to that storage unit. We know they didn't follow us there."

"We also know they didn't have a clue about that place before we got there, or they would've already paid it a visit." He drummed his thumbs on the steering wheel. "They tracked us there."

"They know this car." Sue flipped down the visor and jerked back from her reflection in the mirror. "You could've told me I looked like a raccoon with black circles of ash under my eyes."

He reached across her and grabbed a tissue from the glove compartment. "When would they have had time to bug this car? At the hotel? I don't think they ever knew we were there."

"Maybe not until The Falcon showed up on our doorstep. Don't forget, they know where I live. They could've been bugging your car when you were parked at my place when we were in there cleaning up."

"If they were there when we were, they would've made a move." Hunter scratched the sexy stubble on his chin. "We never found a phone on The Falcon, did we?"

"Nope. We found very little except for that piece of paper in her shoe. Do you think the people who ambushed and beat her have her phone?"

"Makes sense. It also makes sense that The Falcon would have a tracker on every burner phone you picked up, so that she could keep tabs on you."

Sue snatched up the phone in the console, buzzed down the window and tossed it outside onto the highway. "Not anymore."

"It was just a suggestion."

"A damned good one." She patted the dashboard. "But this car is next. Too bad you didn't snag any bug finders in the unit, but I'll get my hands on one and we can sweep this car."

"I'll do one better." He swerved off the highway and pulled in to a gas station. He parked next to the air-and-water station. "Give me some light while I check."

She followed him out of the car and crouched beside him as he scanned the undercarriage. The beam of light from her cell phone followed his hands while he felt for a device.

He rose to his feet, brushing off his jeans. "Nothing."

"They can be pretty small these days. We'll do a more thorough check when we have a device."

"Or I can just swap the car out tomorrow and own up to the cracked dashboard."

"Either way." She pointed to the convenience store. "I need something to drink to soothe my throat. How about you?"

"A couple of gallons of water should do the trick." He coughed and spit into the dirt. "Hotel, right? Unless you want to go back home."

"I'm not going back home until we settle this issue. I feel safer in the hotel—I feel safer with you."

As they drove back to the hotel sipping on their drinks, Sue flipped through the folders on her lap. "It doesn't look like Denver was working with The Falcon, but she definitely knew what he was up to."

"I wonder why she didn't come forward in some way and clear him?"

"We're talking about The Falcon here." Sue gripped her knees. "This is the person who told me to walk away from you forever and then ordered me to send my son away. If it served her purposes to hang Denver out to dry, then she'd do it. The ends justified the means for her."

"I wonder if the hospital and the police identified her yet. Would her fingerprints come back to the Agency?"

"I don't know. If someone's that deep undercover, I can't imagine their ID is going to be easy to ascertain in a situation like this." Sue's fingers curled into her jeans. "It's kind of sad, really. She must have family somewhere—even if that family doesn't include a spouse and children."

"She was at least your father's age. Maybe she had the family first, and with her children grown, she went undercover."

Sue shrugged. "Obviously, I'm not the one to ask. I didn't even know The Falcon was female."

Hunter pulled in to the hotel and left the car with the valet. On the ride up the elevator, he asked, "Do you think our arsonists believe we're dead and gone?"

"I'm sure that was their intent. They must've realized when we went to that storage unit that we were after The Falcon's files—and we led them right to it."

"I'm wondering what they were going to use that explosive device for originally. They couldn't have known before they arrived about the storage unit."

"That's why I'm glad we're here." Sue stepped off the elevator. "It's a little more complicated for them to bomb a whole hotel than one townhouse in Georgetown."

As she flicked out her key card, Hunter cinched his fingers around her wrist. "Wait. It's not that difficult to wire one room in a hotel."

She stepped back while Hunter crouched down and inspected the space under the door. He ran his finger along the seam where the door met the floor and then put his eye to the doorjamb.

"If they think we're dead, they wouldn't be rigging our hotel room, would they?"

"Do they think we're dead?"

Hunter slipped his card into the door and Sue found herself holding her breath as the green lights flashed.

Again, Hunter blocked her entrance, stepping into the room before her. "Looks fine."

Sue followed him in and strode to the window and yanked the drapes closed. "They've upped their game. They're no longer interested in questioning me. They know I've been on the other side all this time, and now they want me dead."

"They also want any information you and The Falcon collected on them all these years. And thanks to your quick thinking—" he drilled a knuckle into the file folder she'd placed on the desk "—you have it and they don't."

Sue rubbed a spot of soot on her jeans. "I'm going to take a shower and wash the smoke and ash away, and then let's see if The Falcon's information can clear me and Denver at the same time."

"And stop whatever this group has planned because that's why both of you got involved in the first place." Hunter pulled out his wallet. "I need another soda. Do you want one?"

"Yes, please. Do you think hot tea would be better?" She stroked her neck and swallowed.

"I don't know about you, but I don't think I could take a hot drink right now."

"You're probably right. Diet for me." She grabbed her pajamas and went into the bathroom.

In the shower, she turned her back to the warm spray and let it pound her neck. She'd been on such a roller coaster these past few days, she couldn't wait for the ride to stop. And when it did, would Hunter be interested in being more than just Drake's father?

Today he'd talked about custody and child support as if they'd be living apart instead of together as a family, which was what she wanted. She'd already wasted too much time with her misplaced priorities, robbing Hunter and Drake both of a relationship with each other.

She loved Hunter. She'd felt ridiculous admitting that to herself years ago when she'd left him. But the years hadn't dissipated her feelings, and when she saw him again in that other hotel room, she knew they were for real.

He'd made it clear—up until the point when he found out about Drake—that he still had strong feelings for her, had never forgotten their time together in Paris. But now?

He seemed to have settled down. The anger had left his blue eyes, but it might return when he met Drake and realized all that he'd missed.

And he'd take out that anger on her—rightly so. She'd been duped, manipulated, and with her puppet master dead, she may also be charged with treason.

The bathroom door cracked open and Hunter

stuck his hand through the space, clutching a can of diet soda. "What are you doing in there?"

"Thinking." She shut off the water. "I'll be right out."

She dried off quickly and slipped into her pajamas. Hunter hadn't made a move to join her in the shower or even joke about it. Yeah, that resentment still simmered beneath the surface of his seeming acceptance of her deception.

She entered the other room, drying her hair with a towel. "You should've seen the drain in the shower—black. We're lucky to be alive."

"Amen." He snapped the tab on her soda can and handed it to her. "I was looking through the files and The Falcon's shorthand is kinda cryptic. I hope you can make more sense out of it than I can. She liked codes, didn't she?"

"Always felt memorized codes were the safest way to communicate." She sat on the bed cross-legged, fluffing a couple of pillows behind her. She patted the space beside her. "Bring those over here and let's have a look. Can you bring our laptops, also? I want to compare any notes I have with hers, and maybe we can fill in more of your chart."

He plucked his T-shirt away from his body. "It's only fair that I shower, too, now that you're all fresh and clean."

"How considerate of you." She crooked her finger. "Can you drop off the files and my laptop on your way to the bathroom?"

He complied and shut the door behind him.

Sue stared at the closed door—another sign that he wanted to keep his distance.

She took another sip of soda, allowing it to pool in the back of her throat, before opening the top file marked Denver Assignment.

As she ran her finger down The Falcon's notes, someone pounded on the hotel door. Her finger froze midpage.

This had better not be another member of the housekeeping staff with laundry.

The pounding resumed before she could even roll off the bed. On her way to the door, her gaze darted to the bathroom, her step faltering.

A split second later, Hunter burst through the door, tucking a towel around his waist. "Don't answer it, especially without your weapon."

He made a detour to the credenza and swept up his gun. He approached the door from the side, his weapon at the ready. Bracing his hand against the door, he leaned in to peer through the peephole. His shoulders dropped. "It's Ryan."

"Who?" Sue stood behind Hunter's broad back, her arms folded, hands bunching the sides of her pajama top.

"Ryan Mesner, my CIA contact."

With his gun still raised, Hunter eased open the door. "You're alone?"

"Not for long. Let me in, Hunter. This is important."

Hunter swung open the door and a tall man with cropped dark hair and a full beard pushed past him.

He leveled a finger at Sue. "Are you Sue Chandler?"

"Yes."

"You'd better get the hell out of here. CIA internal investigations is on its way—and they're prepared to charge you with treason."

Chapter Sixteen

Sue's legs wouldn't move. Her brain wouldn't work. The only thing racing through her mind was that if she were arrested, she'd lose Drake. She couldn't lose Drake.

"They're on their way now?" Hunter dragged some clothes from his suitcase and stepped into a pair of jeans underneath his towel, dropping it to the floor.

"They were just at her place in Georgetown, and now they're triangulating her cell phone."

Sue lunged across the bed and ripped her phone from its charger. She turned it off and stuffed it into her purse.

Hunter pulled a shirt over his head and stuffed his feet into his shoes. "Do they know she's with me?"

"As far as I know they do not, but they've been questioning Ned Tucker. Does he know about you?"

"Ned won't tell them anything. If they went to my place first, Ned didn't tell them I was at this hotel. He's not going to tell them about Hunter."

As she and Hunter shoveled their clothes and toiletries into their bags, she turned to Ryan. "Why are you doing this for me? I don't even know you."

"I've had to watch Major Rex Denver, the most honorable man I know, get dragged through the mud and set up. I'm not going to stand by and watch it happen again to someone who might be able to clear his name."

"And we're not going to allow you to take the fall for this, Ryan. Get the hell out of here now." Hunter clasped Ryan on the shoulder and gave him a shove toward the door.

As Ryan grasped the door handle, Sue grabbed his arm. "Is there any way they can track you here or find out you warned me?"

"I don't have my phone on me, I took a taxi over here and paid cash, and I made sure my face was hidden as I went through the hotel—just in case they decide to check the footage."

"You're a good agent, Ryan. Thanks—you won't regret this. I'm no traitor."

"Neither is Major Denver." He flipped up his hoodie and slid out the door.

"The files." Hunter tipped his head toward the bed. "For God's sake, don't forget those files."

Sue gathered them up and shoved them into the outside pocket of her suitcase. She waited at the door with their bags, as Hunter cleared out the safe and gave the room a once-over. "If they decide to run prints on this room, they're going to ID me."

"Maybe you should stay here and wait for them. I can knock you on the head, and you can pretend you know nothing about any of this." Her voice hitched in her throat. "Drake's going to need one parent who's not in federal prison."

"Nobody's going to prison, and I'm not gonna allow you to bash me over the head." He joined her at the door and held it open. "Now let's get the hell out of Dodge."

They avoided the lobby on their way down to the car and Hunter waved off the valet to load their bags in the trunk himself.

As he pulled away from the hotel, he said, "I'm returning this car now. I don't want anything to be traced back to me, but we can't use your car, either."

"Thanks to The Falcon, we have some options. I've never had to use it before, but there's a safe house near Virginia Beach. I think we'll find everything we need there for a quick getaway."

"How far is Virginia Beach?"

"About four hours."

"We can't drive for four hours in this car. The rental car company most likely has a GPS on this vehicle, and once the CIA shows up, they'll track the car for them."

"I have a plan for that, too." She held up one of her many burner phones. "I'm going to call a friend of mine to pick us up at the airport after you leave the car there. She'll let us have her car and she can take a taxi home."

"Is this Dani from the bar?"

"Dani's on a road trip. This is another friend who owes me and I'm about to collect, big time."

While Hunter drove to the airport, keeping one eye on his rearview mirror, Sue placed a call to her friend.

Jacqueline answered after three rings, her voice sleepy and befuddled. "Hello?"

"Jacqueline, it's Sue. I need your help."

Her words worked like a slap to the face. Jacqueline's voice came back sharp and urgent. "Anything."

"Meet me at Reagan as soon as you can. I'll be at parking lot D, the main entrance. Bring your junker. I'm going to take that car and you'll take a taxi home. I'll pay you for everything—the car, the ride home, your time."

"I'll do it and you don't owe me a dime. You know that, Sue. I'm leaving now."

"And if anyone comes by later and asks you about me…"

"I never got this call."

Sue closed the phone and tossed it out the window. "Like you said—Jeffrey and his gang probably have The Falcon's phone and she may have put trackers in all my burner phones."

"What did you do for this woman that she's willing to leave her home in the middle of the night, drive to the airport and give you her car?"

Sue lifted her shoulders. "I saved her life."

She directed Hunter to the parking lot where he plucked a ticket from the machine. He parked on an upper level, and they emptied the car.

Hunter pulled a T-shirt from his bag and wiped

down the inside of the car for good measure. "They don't have to know you were in this car."

Sue grabbed his wrist as he stuffed the shirt back into his suitcase. "You don't have to do this, Hunter. I can take it from here."

"I'm not leaving you to finish this on your own." He kicked the side of her suitcase. "Besides, you finally have what I came here seeking—information about Denver, and I'm not giving up on that, either."

She pressed her lips against the side of his arm. "I knew you were someone I could count on the minute I met you. I'm just sorry you couldn't count on me."

"I'm counting on you now. I'm counting on you to get us out of this mess and to that safe house."

They dragged their bags and the rest of their gear to the elevator and got off on the ground level. They stationed themselves near the parking arm, turning away each time a car rolled through.

Thirty minutes later, a small compact flashed its lights and pulled to a stop in front of them.

"That's her?" Hunter squinted into the back window.

"That's Jacqueline."

Jacqueline hopped out of the car and ran to Sue. She threw her arms around her, and Sue hugged her back with all her might.

"Thank you so much, Jacqueline."

She flicked her long fingernails in the air. "What else would I do when you call?"

"Jacqueline, this is my friend—no names, just in case."

Jacqueline extended her hand. "Bonjour, no name."

Hunter sketched a bow and kissed her long fingers, befitting the Frenchwoman. "Bonjour. What exactly did Sue do to warrant this loyalty?"

"This?" Jacqueline flicked back her dark hair. "This is nothing compared to what she did for me. She saved my life."

"Okay, I won't ask." He held up his hands. "Could you please open the trunk...if it opens?"

"The remote doesn't open it anymore, but there's always the old-fashioned way." Jacqueline shoved the key into the trunk and lifted it.

As Hunter loaded their bags, Sue took Jacqueline's hands. "Everything still okay with you?"

"Perfect." Jacqueline lifted her delicate brows. "I won't ask the same, but it looks like you have a big, strong man on your side now."

"I do. I'll call you when this is all over."

"Is it ever over for you, Sue?" Jacqueline shook her head. "You give too much."

"This time you gave to me and saved *my* life." She kissed Jacqueline's cheek. "Now call up a car so you're not waiting out here alone. We can't wait with you."

"I'll be fine. I've faced worse than a dark corner at night, and you know it."

They hugged again and Hunter waved. He got behind the wheel of the little car that could, and Sue slipped into the passenger's seat.

Sue directed Hunter back to the highway, heading south, and they drove in silence for a few minutes before he turned to her. "Are you going to tell me how you saved her life, or is that top secret, too?"

"Jacqueline was seeing a dangerous, violent man. The more she tried to get away from him, the more ferociously he went after her, and protective orders did nothing to stop him because he had diplomatic immunity here. But I finally stopped him."

"How?"

"I knew he'd been supplying information about some of his country's dealings to sources who were then using that intel against his country to strike favorable deals." She shoved her hands beneath her thighs. "I told his country."

"What happened to him?"

"I don't know. He disappeared and Jacqueline never heard from him or saw him again."

Hunter whistled. "Do you think he was killed? Was it one of *those* countries?"

She glanced at him out of the corner of her eye. "*Any* country can be one of those kinds of countries."

"I suppose you're right. The US has had our share of spies working against us, but it looks like we're dealing with corruption at the highest levels here. I guess anything is possible." He held out his phone to her. "Are you going to put the address in my GPS or am I going to drive blindly into the night in a car that's on its last legs...wheels?"

"There is no address, or at least not that I'm aware of, but I have the directions up here." She tapped her forehead.

"Then take me home, but when we stop for gas,

I'm going to need some coffee and some food. We haven't had anything to eat since that late lunch, and we've been through an explosion and a whirlwind escape from the hotel."

"Let me know if you want me to drive." Sue curled one leg beneath her. "I hope The Falcon's files have enough to prove my innocence. Someone at the Agency *has* to know what she was doing. With all the money and support we had, she couldn't have been running a rogue operation."

"And her black ops contact at the CIA can't be our insider, or he never would've allowed her to compile the information she got."

Sue shivered. "That's a scary thought—the one person who can verify The Falcon's existence is the one working with this terrorist group."

"I have a feeling the insider is terrified of black ops groups like The Falcon's. Those groups are the very ones that could uncover a leak or a spy within."

"There's just one problem."

"What?"

"Why hasn't this person stepped forward yet?"

"The Falcon just died this afternoon. Her contact may not even know that yet." Hunter squeezed her knee. "It'll be okay, Sue. I'm not gonna let this end any other way—I've got a son to meet."

They drove through the night, stopping for gas, coffee and snacks. As they began to head east, toward the coast, Sue studied the road signs and the landmarks.

She'd never been to this safe house before, but The

Falcon had drilled its location along with countless other details into Sue's head for so long, she felt as if she'd been this way before.

"Here, here, here." She hit the window with the heel of her hand. "Turn right here."

"Are you sure?" Hunter turned the wheel, anyway. "It looks dark and deserted. I hope you're not directing me right into the water."

"The isolation is the point...and the water is farther out with a few more houses scattered out there." She hunched forward in her seat, gripping the edge of the dashboard. "Turn left at the big tree. It should be a gravel road—not quite unpaved."

The little car bounced and weaved as they hit the gravel, but the headlights picked out a clapboard house ahead with a wooden porch.

"That's it. I think you can park around the back."

The car crawled around the side of the house and Hunter cut the engine. "Let's leave the stuff in the car so we can check it out first. I suppose you know where to find the key."

"Exactly." She took his cell phone because she was running out of ones of her own and she hadn't had a chance to charge the temp phone she'd picked up at the gas station. She turned on the flashlight and stepped from the car.

Several feet from the house, she spotted the rock garden and she lit up the ground below her to avoid tripping over the uneven surface. She counted three rocks from the left and crouched before it, digging her fingers in the dirt to tip it over.

Bugs scurried at the invasion while she sifted the dirt with her fingers. "Got it."

She pulled the key free from its hiding place and wiped it clean on the thigh of her jeans.

She returned to Hunter waiting by the car, his gun drawn. She pointed to the weapon dangling by his side. "Expecting company?"

"You never know."

She held up the key in the light. "I think this works on the back door, too."

Hunter dogged her steps as she walked to the back of the small house and unlocked the back door.

She pushed open the door, clenching her jaw. Something had to go right. This had to work. Creeping to the front of the house with Hunter right behind her, she held the phone in front of her. She sniffed, the musty odor making her nose twitch.

Hunter voiced her thoughts. "Hasn't been used for a while, has it?"

"Doesn't smell like it, but then I think this particular place was sitting in reserve for me and I never needed it...until now." She twisted on the switch for a lamp centered on an end table and a yellow glow illuminated the comfortable furniture.

"Looks more like my nana's place than a spy hideaway." Hunter picked up a throw pillow, punched it once and dropped it back onto the sofa.

"That's the point." Sue wandered into the kitchen and flicked on the light. "It's supposed to be stocked—with all kinds of things."

Hunter crowded into the kitchen next to her and

tugged open the fridge. "Not much in here. Bottled water, which I could actually use right now."

Sue reached past him to open the cupboard door. She shuffled through some cans of food and freeze-dried pouches. "This is more like it. Stuff for the long haul. I don't know how often these safe house supplies are replenished."

Hunter leaned over her shoulder and picked up one of the packets and threw it back into the cupboard. "Ugh, looks like an MRE. I'll pass on these for the local pizza joint."

Sue returned to the living room and turned in a circle, her hand on her hip. She'd seen this room and knew just where to look.

"Do you have a knife on you?"

Hunter reached for his belt and produced a switchblade. "What do you need?"

Sue knelt in front of the fireplace and lifted the braided rug. She placed her hand on the wood slats and rocked back and forth. When she felt some give, she pounded the board with her fist. "Here. Try here."

Hunter crouched beside her and jimmied the blade of his knife between the two slats. When he got a lip on one, he pulled it up to reveal a cavity in the floor.

He scooted onto his belly and put his face to the space. "There's a canvas bag in there, along with a few spiders. We'll need a bigger space to bring it up."

Sue curled her hand around the next slat and yanked it free. They had to dislodge one more before they were able to lift the bag from the space beneath the floor.

Hunter swung it out and plopped it onto the floor.

Sue eyed it, wrinkling her nose. "Are those spiders gone?"

"Badass spy like you worried about a few spiders?"

"Yes."

Hunter kicked the bag a few times. "That should do it. Are you sure it's not booby-trapped?"

"Why would there be a booby-trapped bag in a *safe* house?"

"I have no idea how you people operate, but just in case, I'll let you open it first."

"What a man." She pinched his side.

Leaning over, she unzipped the bag and peeled back the canvas. She clicked her tongue as she ran her hands through the stacks of cash. "Nice. Having all this means never having to use your credit card."

She dug in deeper and pulled out a gun. "Untraceable I'm sure."

Hunter dived in next to her and withdrew handfuls of minicameras, GPS trackers, a small flashlight. "This is a mini stash of the same stuff she had in the storage unit."

"Minus the fire suits." Sue rubbed her arms and looked around the room. "I hope we don't need those here."

Hunter scooted back, sitting on the floor and leaning his back against the sofa. "We can stay here for a few days and catch our breath. Really look over The Falcon's files on Denver and this whole assignment and get your name cleared once and for all. Get you back to Drake where you belong."

"Which reminds me." Sue held up one finger. "I need to get that phone charged so I can call my parents tomorrow morning, just to make sure everything's okay. I suppose I'm going to have to tell my father that I'm under investigation. I'm sure the CIA investigators are going to pay them a visit."

"Maybe not. They might be afraid of tipping off your parents and having them shield you and hide you."

"Funny thing is? They probably wouldn't."

"It's late, Sue. I'm going to bring in our bags and then you're going to get some sleep."

"You, too."

"Yeah, of course."

She narrowed her eyes. "Right. You have no intention of sleeping, do you? You're going to be on guard all night long."

"I'll catch some shut-eye. Don't worry about me." He stood up and made for the back door.

Sue zipped up the bag and dragged it next to the fireplace. The day's events caught up to her and she sank onto the sofa. She didn't even blink when Hunter came through the back door, hauling their suitcases.

The sofa dipped as he sat beside her, pulling her against his chest. "Do you think the beds are made up?"

She murmured against his shirt, "I don't care at this point. I'm going to fall asleep right here."

He kissed her temple. "Stay right here."

Sue must've drifted off. It seemed like hours later when Hunter returned and took off her shoes, lifted her legs to the sofa and spread a blanket over her body.

He sat back down in the corner and shifted over so that her head nestled on his lap, as he stroked her temple.

A smile curved her lips. Whatever happened now, she could endure it as long as Hunter stayed right by her side.

Chapter Seventeen

Her lashes fluttered, and she reached for Hunter. When her hand met the sofa cushion instead of the warm flesh she'd expected, she bolted upright.

"I'm in here." Hunter waved from the kitchen across the room. "I'm making oatmeal if you're interested, but we have to skip the bananas, blueberries, almonds, brown sugar and everything else that makes it remotely tasty."

"Breakfast?" Sue rubbed her eyes, running her tongue along her teeth, which she'd been too tired to brush last night. "I didn't even realize it was morning."

"You slept soundly."

"Did you sleep at all?" She gathered her hair into a ponytail.

"A little." He held up the burner phone she'd bought yesterday. "It's fully charged, and better yet, it's not being tracked by The Falcon."

She yawned and shrugged off the blanket. "I wonder who pays the utility bills for this place to keep the gas, water and electricity running."

"Probably comes from some supersecret spy slush fund."

She joined him in the kitchen and watched him stir hot water into some instant oatmeal. "Not bad. I'll have some of this coffee first, though."

She leaned her elbows on the counter and plucked the phone from the charger. She entered her father's cell phone number, although at this point it might be worse talking to him than Linda.

"Hi, Dad."

Hunter held a finger to his lips. He didn't want her to give Dad the lowdown on her situation in case the CIA hadn't contacted them yet.

"Hi, Sue." Her father didn't even ask her about the new phone number. He knew. "Drake's just fine, although he misses his...cousins."

Sue's shoulders sagged. For a minute, she thought Drake had been missing her. "I hope you're keeping him busy. He likes blocks and he loves riding his tricycle."

"He sure is an active boy." Dad cleared his throat. "We had a surprise this morning."

"Oh?" Sue's heart picked up speed.

"A friend of yours named Dani Howard called and asked if she could stop by for a visit. Says her daughter plays with Drake there in DC?"

Sue patted her chest and sucked in a breath. "That's right. She told me she was driving down to Savannah to visit her folks and said she'd stop in to see Drake."

"Okay, just checking. She's going to call back, and I'll tell her it's fine."

"Thanks, Dad." She threw a quick glance at Hunter, pouring a cup of coffee. "Sh-should you put Drake on the line? I'll say a quick hi."

"He's outside on that trike already, Sue. Maybe later. This a new number for you?"

"For the time being. Don't program it in your phone or label it."

"I know better."

Sue's mind flashed back to her father's fake passports in The Falcon's storage unit. *I bet you do.*

"Okay, then. Just keep me posted. Everything else…all right?"

"Everything's just fine. We'll have Drake back at Amelia's just as soon as they return from the Bahamas."

"Maybe he'll be returning to me instead."

Hunter's hand pouring the condensed milk jerked and he splashed milk on the counter.

Her father paused for several seconds. "Why would you say that? Mission over? Won't there be another?"

"We'll talk about it later. Just keep my little boy safe." She ended the call and tucked the phone into her purse.

"Drake's okay?" Hunter shoved a cup of coffee at her.

"He's fine. Apparently, he's always just fine without me." She blew on the coffee before sipping it.

"You meant what you said to your father? That Drake will be going back home with you?"

"The Falcon's dead. These assignments, this life-style I have is too dangerous for a parent. As soon as I'm clear, I'm done."

He scooped up a spoonful of oatmeal and studied it. "I'm not arrogant enough to tell you what to do, but I think it's a good idea—if you can manage it."

"I have to get out of this mess first, or Drake will be visiting me behind bars—both of us."

After two more tastes, Hunter gave up on the lumpy oatmeal and dropped the bowl into the sink. "Who's driving down to Savannah and stopping in to see Drake?"

"My friend Dani Howard. She has a daughter around Drake's age."

"Is she the one you went out with the night you ran into Jeffrey?"

"Same. Thank God he left her alone. Jeffrey's co-hort must've had orders not to hurt her."

"Does Dani know what you do for a living?" Hunter rinsed out the bowl and held out his hand for hers.

"I'm willing to give it a try." She yanked the bowl back and held it to her chest. "Dani? Yeah, she knows I'm with the Agency but not much more, of course."

"And what does she do?"

"She's a nurse." Sue wrapped her hands around her bowl and walked to her suitcase. She unzipped the outside pocket and pulled out the file folders she'd rescued from fire and mayhem.

"I think it's time for me to have a good long look at these and try to decipher The Falcon's notes. They're my only chance right now."

She brought the files to the kitchen table, and as she dropped them, the contents spilled out of one of them. She pinched a newspaper clipping between two fingers and she waved it in the air. "From a French newspaper, but it looks old. Probably nothing to do with Denver."

"You read French, don't you?"

"Oui, oui." She pulled up a chair and scooted under the table. She brought the article close to her face, translating out loud a story about a bombing in a Paris café that took the lives of four people, one a child.

When she finished reading, Sue pressed the article to her heart. "How awful. This sounds familiar."

"It's all too familiar." He leaned over her shoulder and plucked up another article. "Looks like it could be the same story."

She took it from his fingers and scanned it. "Yes, the same story, different newspaper or maybe a follow-up."

Straddling the chair next to her, Hunter asked, "Why was she keeping this story in particular? She must've worked a lot of these types of cases."

"Maybe she has more articles on more cases, but I didn't happen to pick those up."

"But these were filed in the same cabinet as the Denver material." Hunter rubbed his chin and shuffled through the folder. He slid another article toward him with his forefinger. "This one has an accompanying picture."

He squinted at the two women and one man, grim-faced, looking away from the camera. "What's this one say, Sue?"

Her gaze flicked over the words. "They're the victims, or the victims' family members."

"Sue," Hunter bumped her shoulder with his as he ducked over the article. "Doesn't that look like a young Falcon? And I don't mean the bird."

"What? No." She smoothed her thumb across the pinched face of a woman, her sharp chin dipping to her chest. "This one?"

"Exactly." He circled her face with his fingertip. "You said The Falcon didn't have a family. How'd you know that?"

"When she was telling me how I needed to leave you and then give up Drake, she implied that this job and a family didn't mix. I just assumed she was speaking from experience."

He tapped the picture. "Maybe she *was* speaking from experience. Maybe she lost her daughter in that explosion."

"And her husband." Sue pressed a hand against her roiling belly. "The child killed in the blast had the same last name as one of the men who died."

Hunter blew out a breath that stirred the edges of the clippings. "It makes sense, doesn't it? If she lost her own family to a terrorist attack, maybe one that was directed at her and her loved ones, she'd want to warn you away from that possibility."

"I feel sick to my stomach."

"I wonder why she put this personal stuff with the Denver notes."

"Maybe it's more than personal. Do you think The Falcon has been tracking this group for—" she glanced at the date on the newspaper "—twenty years?"

Hunter pointed at the articles. "Did they ever find out who was responsible? Or more likely, did anyone take credit for the attack?"

Sue flipped through the rest of the articles. "Nidal al Hamed's group claimed responsibility. That group is the precursor to Al Tariq, but more importantly al Hamed's son broke away from Al Tariq a few years ago to form his own organization—an international organization that finds common bonds with terrorists across the globe, no matter what their agenda."

"The Falcon's entire investigation could be a personal vendetta."

"You can frame it that way, but this group has hurt more than just The Falcon's family."

"Nidal's dead, right? What's his son's name?"

Sue cranked her head to the side, her eyes as big as saucers. "Walid. Walid al Hamed."

"From the barbershop." Hunter slapped his hand on the table.

"It's not an uncommon name. Don't jump to conclusions."

"Could the leader of this new group be hiding out in plain sight in the middle of DC, mere miles from CIA headquarters?" Hunter swung his leg over the chair and paced to the window, the drapes firmly pulled across them.

"And this could be the same group Denver is tracking. The two investigations must converge somewhere in here." She fanned out the pages of the Denver folder on the table.

"You worked with The Falcon, knew her fondness for codes. Get on it, girl." Hunter strode toward his laptop on the coffee table. "I'm going to research something else that's been bugging me."

"What?"

"How long have you known Dani Howard?" Hunter sat on the sofa and flipped open his laptop.

The pen Sue had poised over a blank piece of paper fell from her fingers. "What? Why? I've known Dani for almost two years."

"Where did you meet her?"

Sue forgot about the articles and her research and turned around, fully facing Hunter. "At the pediatrician. We both had our kids in at the same time. Drake had an ear infection. Why are you asking these questions about Dani? You were probing me about her before when I got off the phone."

"I just thought it was unusual for her to take a detour from her trip to Savannah to see your parents. I mean, if you were there, I could see it."

"Sh-she just thought a familiar face from home would be nice for Drake."

"Why? He's at his grandparents', and excuse me for saying this, but isn't he more at home in South

Carolina than he is here?" He held up a hand. "I don't mean to poke at you or criticize."

"Yeah, but I didn't think her offer was weird. Do you?" She scooted to the edge of her chair, her heart beating double time. "How long have you been thinking about this?"

"It niggled at me after your conversation with your father." He tapped his keyboard, and without looking up, he asked, "Whose idea was it to go out that night and who picked the bar?"

"Dani, but she was always the one issuing the invitations and she goes out more than I do, so it's only natural for her to pick the spot."

"And who noticed the two men that night?"

Sue sprang from her chair, gripping her arms, her fingers digging into her flesh. "Stop it. You're scaring me."

"Who noticed the two men, Sue?"

"Dani." She locked her knees so they'd stop wobbling. "Of course she did. That was her thing."

"Was it also her thing to leave with men when you two were out together, or was that an unusual move for her that night?"

"It was atypical, but that was a different kind of night. We were drugged. I don't think she realized what she was doing." Sue pressed a hand against her forehead. "This is crazy. She has a young daughter. I've been in her home. She has pictures of…of…"

Hunter glanced up sharply from his laptop. "Of what?"

"Of her daughter."

He hunched forward on his elbows. "And what else?"

"I don't know." She sat next to him on the sofa. "Maybe it's what she didn't have, or maybe you're just making me crazy for no reason at all."

"What didn't she have?"

"She had pictures of Fiona but nobody else— no family photos. I know she didn't get along with her mother." She flicked her finger at the computer screen. "What have you been looking up?"

"Did a general search of Dani Howard, and I didn't find much. What hospital does she work at?"

"She doesn't work at a hospital. She works for a medical group."

"Do you know the name of it? I'll look it up." He gestured to her phone on the kitchen counter. "Call it."

"It's Mercer Medical. I've picked her up there before." She jogged across the room to grab her phone.

"Out front or did you go inside?" His fingers moved quickly across his keyboard.

Sue licked her dry lips. "Outside only, but she had a lab coat on."

"You mean like the one you stole in the hospital yesterday? Call." He swung his computer around to face her. "The website doesn't list any personnel."

"I know Dani. You don't. I think you're on the wrong track here." She entered the number on the website with trembling fingers.

Hunter said, "Speaker."

She tapped the speaker button just as someone

picked up the phone. "Mercer Medical, how may I direct your call?"

"I'm trying to reach a nurse there, Dani Howard."

The pause on the other end seemed to last a lifetime. "What doctor does she work for? He?"

"Dani is a she. Dr. Warner."

"She doesn't work for Dr. Warner. Is she new?"

Sue squeezed the phone in her hand. "C-could you check. Maybe it's not Dr. Warner. Could she be in another office?"

"I'll check, ma'am, but this is the only Mercer office in the DC area."

Sue heard some clicking on the other end, which sounded like pickaxes against rock. Her gaze met Hunter's, but if she expected reassurance, what she saw was grim confirmation instead.

The receptionist came back on the line. "I'm sorry, ma'am. There's no Dani Howard here. Perhaps you…"

Sue didn't hear what she should perhaps do because she ended the call and dropped to the edge of the coffee table. "Oh my God. What have I done?"

"You've done nothing." Hunter placed a steadying hand on her bouncing knee. "Call your father right now and warn him against Dani. He'll know what to do."

Sue went back to her phone and called her father for the second time that morning, this time putting the call on speaker for Hunter.

"Hello?" Leave it to Dad to know not to assume

it was her calling just because it was the same number from this morning.

"Dad, it's Sue again."

"Don't worry. Drake is fine."

She flattened a hand against her fluttering belly. "I need to tell you something very important. That woman who's supposed to come by..."

"Yeah, Dani. Nice girl."

The blood in Sue's veins turned to ice. "She's there? Dad..."

"No, they're not here. Dani and her little girl Fiona took Drake to the park down the street."

Chapter Eighteen

A sharp pain pierced the back of his head, but Hunter didn't have time to succumb to it. Sue had dropped the phone and let out a wail.

Her father was shouting into the phone. "Sue? Sue? What's wrong?"

Hunter scooped up the phone. "Mr. Chandler, I'm with Sue right now. Dani Howard isn't who she says she is. When did they leave? Can you catch up to them?"

Sue's father swore. "We didn't know. How were we supposed to know? They left over thirty minutes ago."

"Did you see her car?"

"Of course I did. Who the hell are you, anyway?"

"I'm Sue's…friend. I'm trying to help her, and she needs help. The Falcon is dead and Sue's been implicated. She has no one to vouch for her and now they've taken Drake."

"The hell they have. I'll get him back. You tell my little girl. Tell her I'll get him back. I'm going out right now. Our town isn't that big. Someone must've seen them."

"While you do, stay on the phone with me and tell me everything you remember about Dani and her car."

As Mr. Chandler gave him the details of Dani's visit, Hunter squeezed Sue's shoulder. She hadn't moved since getting the news from her father, except to drop her head in her hands.

Sue's stepmother interrupted her husband.

"What are you saying, Linda? Phone number?"

"What is it, sir?"

"My wife said that snake, Dani, left her a new phone number for Sue. Said she'd lost her phone on the road and picked up a temporary one. She wanted Sue to have the number." Chandler snorted. "I'll bet she did."

"Give me the number. It's probably the contact phone for Sue's instructions."

Sue's father recited the number to him. "What do they want with Sue, anyway?"

"I think they just want Sue."

Sue moaned. "They can have me as long as they let Drake go."

Sue's father yelled into the phone. "Don't be ridiculous, Sue. Do you know what they'll do to you? Someone who betrayed them? Someone who has information about them?"

"I'd rather have them do it to me than Drake."

Hunter knelt beside her and brushed the hair from

her hot face. "We'll get him back. Don't worry. Your father gave me some good information."

Mr. Chandler said, "I'm already in my car. I'm going to find her. I'll keep you posted."

Hunter ended the call and ran his hand over Sue's back. "We're going to rescue him, but we'll play along. Call Dani now. She won't be expecting you to call her for a while—not until your parents notify you that she never brought Drake home."

Sue straightened her spine and pulled back her shoulders. "Catch her off guard."

"Exactly."

Sue snatched the phone from his fingers and tapped in the number as he recited it to her from memory. He didn't have to tell her to put it on speaker.

This was his son—a son he'd never even met. He'd go to hell and back to bring him home.

"Yes?"

A woman answered the phone. There was children's laughter in the background, and Hunter ground his teeth. What kind of a mother could kidnap a child from another mother?

Sue's nostrils flared and her cheeks flushed. "Where's my son, you bitch?"

Dani drew in a sharp breath, audible over the line. "That was fast."

"You've had him for half an hour. You can't be far. My father's out looking for you."

"How did he find out?" Dani laughed. "I guess

he's a better CIA operative than you are. You didn't have a clue for almost two years."

"Why would I think another *mother* would be plotting against me?"

Dani clicked her tongue. "Oh, Sue. You don't have to play the outraged mother with me. You're never with Drake anyway, but I hope you care enough to turn yourself over to us to keep him safe."

"Keep your commentary to yourself and tell me what I need to do."

"I'll call you back with instructions. I really didn't expect you to call so quickly—and make sure your parents know that if we detect any police involvement, you'll never see Drake again."

Sue covered her mouth with her hand but didn't let the fear seep into her voice. "Why did you move in on me two years ago? Did Walid al Hamed's group suspect me then?"

The silence on the other end of the line proved that they'd been right about Walid's group being behind the plot.

Dani cleared her throat and recovered. "Nobody knew for sure, but you really should've been spending all that money we'd funneled to you. Once we realized someone was checking out that barbershop, we knew we had you…and your boss, too."

"You killed her."

"We left her for dead. She must've been a tough old bird. We never imagined she'd pull herself together and go see you. And we never imagined you'd get out of that storage unit alive."

"I guess you underestimated both of us."

"Who's your sidekick? Who's helping you?"

Sue reached out and squeezed Hunter's hand. "I work alone. You should know that by now."

"It doesn't matter who he is. You'll be on your own for sure now. Any interference and Drake is gone."

"What does that mean, *gone*?" Sue's body seemed to vibrate.

"You don't want to find out. I'll be in touch."

Dani cut off the call, and Sue's shoulders rounded. "They're going to interrogate me—torture me to find out what I know about the organization, and then they're going to kill me."

Hunter laced his fingers with hers. "Do you think I'm going to allow that to happen? We'll find a way to get Drake back and keep you safe."

"We have to be able to use The Falcon's files to lure them into a change of plans. They don't know what we have, if anything, from that storage unit."

He pushed off the sofa and pulled her along with him. "Then let's get back to those files and see if we can trade anything for Drake."

Sue shuffled the papers from The Falcon's personal folder and closed it, setting it aside. "That's The Falcon's motivation for bringing down this group and now I have my own personal reasons."

"Then let's do it." He slid her notebook and pen in front of him. "What do those notes say about the group Denver is investigating?"

"Looks like The Falcon picked up on Denver's activities a while ago. There was a bombing at a Syrian refugee camp designed to derail the negotiations between the Syrian government and the rebels—it worked. So, Walid's group is all about fomenting dissent in the Middle East…and Africa." She tapped the paper with her finger. "Denver discovered a cache of weapons at an embassy outpost in Nigeria. He's putting these events together like nobody else is and The Falcon is paying attention."

"Someone else was paying attention, too, and that's why he was set up. There has to be someone on the inside."

"At what level?" She skimmed her fingertip down a list of agencies and names. "The Falcon was on that track, also."

"Walid's group, which doesn't even have a name, is dependent on this insider and they're desperate to keep him a secret."

"Then we need to pretend we know who this insider is and that we have the proof to bring him down—and we'll do it unless we get Drake back."

"That won't work, Sue. We can't offer the people who took Drake any insurance that we didn't pass along this info to someone before we collect Drake, or any assurance that we didn't take pictures of the proof with our phones." He rubbed a circle on her back. "The only thing we have as a bargaining chip—is you."

Sue folded her arms and buried her face in the crook of her elbow. "Then it has to be done. My life for Drake's. It's a no-brainer."

"It's a no-brainer that you're going to show up, but I'll figure out a way to get you both out alive." He put his head close to hers and his warm breath stirred her hair. "I found you again and discovered we have a son together. Do you seriously think I'm going to let anything come between me and everything I ever wanted?"

She raised her head and kissed his chin. "How did I ever let myself get talked into leaving you and keeping Drake from you?"

Tapping the notebook with his knuckle, he said, "This is how. The work. Your work."

"And where has that work gotten me? Estranged from you, Drake kidnapped, my career and my very life in jeopardy."

"Make it worthwhile."

"You mean instead of wallowing in self-pity?" She picked up the pen and resumed her examination of The Falcon's notes.

"I know what your problem is, and it's not self-pity." He stood up and made a move toward the kitchen. "You need to eat something. You never finished that awful oatmeal. I'll make us something else awful."

While Hunter banged around in the kitchen, Sue put together a time line of all the events that linked Major Denver with their undercover work with Walid. "It's here. This is it, Hunter. Walid's group is the same one Denver has been tracking and the same one The Falcon had me infiltrate. But for what purpose?"

"What purpose?" He walked toward her carrying two bowls of something steaming.

She sniffed the air. "Chicken noodle soup? Drake loves noodles."

"Must be genetic. This stuff is homemade, straight from the can." He set the soup at her elbow, a spoon already poking up from the bowl. "What purpose are you talking about?"

"The connection between Denver's investigation and the one I was doing with The Falcon is evident, but I don't know why either investigation is so important. This group—" she thumbed through the pages "—really hasn't been up to much of anything. Outside of the Syrian bombing and another in Paris, the group has been operating under the radar."

"Denver seems to think they're plotting something big, and obviously The Falcon thought so, too."

"In the US." Hunter blew on his soup before sucking a noodle into his mouth. "Yeah, I know that."

She shifted her gaze from Hunter's lips and glanced down at the page in front of her. "The Falcon does have *GB* several times on the page. Could there be an impending attack in Great Britain, also? It just doesn't make sense in the context of her notes, which really couldn't be more confusing if she tried."

"GB?" Hunter dropped his spoon and snatched the notes from her hand. "That's what the military calls sarin gas."

Sue choked. "My God, Hunter. That's it. A weapon in the context of these notes makes so much more sense than a place. They're planning a sarin attack. But where?"

She scrambled through The Falcon's notes again, drawing a blank. Slumping in her chair, she dropped the notes onto the table. "Do you think these are enough to clear me with the CIA? There are references to the people I met and why. The Agency can't accuse me of collaborating with the enemy once they see The Falcon's notes. Someone has to come forward at some point to claim The Falcon. She didn't work in a vacuum."

"They'll go a long way toward proving your innocence."

"Then maybe I should turn myself in now. Maybe they can help us get Drake back."

"That would be the worst thing we could do for Drake right now. If there's an insider, and these notes—" he smashed his fist against the papers "—indicate there is, how long do you think it's gonna take him, or her, to report back that the Agency is aware of the kidnapping?"

"Not long at all." She plowed her fingers through her hair and dug her nails into her scalp.

Her cell phone rang and she froze.

Hunter picked up the phone and checked the display. "It's your father."

Sue lunged for the phone. "Dad?"

"I couldn't find her, Sue. I don't know where she took him, but he's gone."

"We'll handle it, Dad. I'll get Drake back."

"At what cost?"

"Whatever it takes."

When her conversation with her father ended, Sue finally picked up her spoon and took a few sips of soup. She'd hoped that The Falcon's notes would contain a blueprint to clear her, clear Denver, give her something to use to bargain with Drake's kidnappers, ID the mole and map out the plan for Walid's attack. It only hinted at some of those things, leaving the rest just out of her grasp.

She cared only about Drake now. His safety was more important than all the rest. It always was and she hadn't been able to see that until now.

Her phone rang again, and when she looked at the calling number, she inhaled her soup so fast it went up her nose. "It must be Dani."

She put it on speaker and answered. "Yes?"

Dani answered, a slight accent creeping into her voice that Sue had never noticed before. "Are you ready?"

"I'm ready for anything."

"You'd better be." Dani spoke away from the phone in a muffled voice and then continued. "We're going to pick you up on a street corner in DC at midnight tonight. If anyone follows us or we see any police presence, helicopters, drones or any other suspicious activity, your son will disappear."

"Are you bringing him with you when you pick me up? How will I know he's safe?"

"We'll let you video chat with him on the phone before we pick you up. We'll even let you see him before before we take you away for interrogation."

Hunter jumped up from the table, his hands clenched into fists.

Sue met his gaze. "How do I know you'll let him go once you have me?"

"You'll just have to trust us. We're working out a plan for your father to pick the boy up."

"I need more than that." Hot anger thumped through her veins and she pressed two fingers against her throbbing temple.

"What choice do you have, Sue? Are you going to be at the meeting place tonight or not?"

Hunter came up behind her and stroked the side of her neck.

Sue took a deep breath and swallowed. "Of course I'll be there. Give me the instructions."

As Dani reeled off the steps, Sue wrote them down on a piece of paper. When the call ended, she dropped her head to that paper and banged her head on the table. "What are we going to do? There's no way to find out where they're going to take me. You can't follow us. She already said they're going to divest me of any cell phones, purses, bags, and they're even leaving clothes for me to change into so I can't sew anything into my clothing. And I don't even know if Drake will be safe at the end of this. They might kill us both."

Hunter braced his hands on the table, his head drooping between his arms. "That's not going to…"

His head jerked up. "Where's the bag from the floor with all the cash?"

"By the fireplace." She jerked her thumb over her shoulder. "Why?"

Crossing to the fireplace in three long strides, he said over his shoulder, "The Falcon had every conceivable spy tool in that storage unit. She also had some in that bag."

"GPS tracker? They'll find it, Hunter."

He knelt before the bag and dived into it, dragging out stacks of money and throwing them over his shoulder. His hands scrabbled through the items in the bottom of the bag, and then he sat back on his heels, with a smile that showed all his white teeth.

"Got it. God bless The Falcon."

"What do you have?" Sue sprang up from her chair like a jack-in-the-box and launched herself at him.

He waved the package in front of her nose. "You're going to swallow the GPS."

Chapter Nineteen

Hunter tugged his hat lower on his forehead as he watched Sue across the street in her ill-fitting jeans and baggy T-shirt. She still looked incredible, regal even, as she awaited her fate—and Drake's.

They'd made the four-hour drive back to DC that afternoon and had lain low in a chain hotel outside the capital until it was time to leave. They'd come separately, he in a disguise, so nobody would make the link between him and Sue.

She'd followed their instructions to the T, picking up a bag at the front desk of the specified hotel, changing into the clothing in the bag, stashing her own clothes, along with any personal items, in the bag and checking it back in with the bellhop.

Now she waited on that corner with no guarantee that her sacrifice would spare Drake. *He* was her guarantee. He finally had the family he'd dreamed of having and he wasn't going to let it—or them— slip out of his grasp so easily.

He brought up the GPS app on his phone and entered the code for the tracker in Sue's belly. She appeared as a stationary green dot.

Sensing movement, Hunter shifted his gaze from his phone to the street. A blue van pulled up alongside Sue and she hopped in. Just like that, she disappeared from his sight, and a wave of panic clutched at his innards for a few seconds until he got his bearings.

They could search her all they wanted; they'd never find the tracker. But he—and they—had to act quickly. It was good for only a few hours, and he couldn't be seen following the van.

He swallowed the fear bubbling up from his gut and paid for his coffee and apple pie. He hobbled out of the twenty-four-hour café and made a sharp turn toward the parking garage where he'd left the car borrowed from Sue's friend.

Nobody knew that car. Nobody knew the bearded man in the Nationals cap with the slight paunch and the stiff leg. He limped toward the elevator, passing a few tourists out on the town, maybe going to their nighttime monuments tour.

When he got behind the wheel of the car, he checked his phone again. Sue and the van were headed out of the city, south toward Virginia.

He followed their path. At this rate, he'd be pulling in to the destination ten minutes after they did. If her captors acted quickly and whisked her or Drake away as soon as they got there, he didn't stand a chance. They didn't even know if Drake would be waiting at the location. He might be somewhere else completely.

He pounded his hands against the steering wheel. He couldn't let himself think that way. He had to be Delta Force right now. He had to remove the personal feelings from this mission and focus on the objective. Rescue the targets and kill the enemy, if necessary.

With his phone propped up on the dashboard, he followed the green bull's-eye. Forty-five minutes passed before the van made a move off the highway. Hunter checked the map and saw farmland. A rural area would expose him, but it would expose them, too.

And he had all the gear he needed to conduct a raid—Delta Force–style.

When the target stopped moving, Hunter caught his breath. He was eight minutes out. As he continued to drive, he pulled up another map on his phone and switched to a street-view image. The location of the green dot matched up to what looked like a barn of some sort.

His mind clicked into action. A barn—high ceilings, wooden structure, possible fire hazard, maybe a hayloft, horse stalls. Places for concealment.

He parked his car a half mile out, hiding it behind a clump of bushes. He secured his backpack, the weight of his equipment solid on his shoulders. He stumbled onto a dirt access road—no trees or cover-up to the structure, but high grass, high enough to conceal a man in a crouching position.

He waded into the grass, hunching forward, his pack bouncing on his back. The vegetation whispered beneath his feet, and he could imagine it said "Sue, Sue" with every step closer to the barn.

Just as he was close enough to emerge from the grass and hit the ground in an army crawl for the ages, Hunter almost plowed into a man standing on the edge of the grass.

Hunter fell to the side just as the guard cocked his head. Hunter circled around to the side, grateful for the wind that kicked up and fluffed the grass, making it sigh.

The man on duty didn't know which way to look, and when he cranked his head in the other direction, away from him, Hunter made his move.

He came from the side, hacked his hand across the man's windpipe to silence any cries, shoved his gun beneath his left rib cage and pulled the trigger.

The silencer made a whooshing sound and the man collapsed to the ground, his blood already soaking the dirt. "That's for Major Denver, you bastard."

Hunter searched him for a walkie or cell phone and found the latter. Hopefully, Hunter would be in that building before anyone decided to check with the guard on watch.

Stashing the dead guard's weapon in his backpack, Hunter dropped to the ground and crawled toward the barn. He paused next to the van and hitched up to his knees.

He pressed his ear against the side of the van, which rumbled with the sound of a radio. Damn—someone waited inside. He'd never make it to the barn without being seen.

He scanned the ground and scraped his fingers through the dirt to collect some pebbles. He tossed these up in the air and they showered down on the top of the van. Then he scrambled beneath the van and held his breath.

The driver's door opened and one booted foot landed in the dirt. Another followed, and the driver emerged from the van, facing it, probably trying to see the roof.

As the man's boot heels eased up off the ground, Hunter rolled out from beneath the van and bashed the guard in the kneecaps.

The man gave a strangled cry and swung his weapon down to point it at his surprise attacker. The same look of shock was stamped on his face when Hunter shot him. "That's for Sue, you bastard."

His path now cleared to the barn, Hunter returned to the ground and snaked his way to the building. When he heard the high, clear tones of a child's voice, his heart lurched.

He was here. His son was here.

The barn's windows were too high to see into and he couldn't charge through that swinging front door without knowing the situation inside first. He crawled around to the side of the building and swung his pack from his shoulder.

He rummaged through the contents, feeling each item with his fingers, identifying each gadget from memory. When his fingertip traced around a small, round object encased in plastic packaging, he withdrew it from the backpack.

This little device could be his eyes inside the barn, give him some situational awareness. He slit the package open with his knife and programmed the spy cam into his phone. He rose, creeping up the side of the barn, and swung his arm at the window above him a few times to judge the distance.

As long as this didn't land on someone's head, he should be able to slip it inside without anyone knowing they were being watched.

Saying a silent prayer, he tossed the minicam through the window and into the barn. He held still for several seconds, his muscles taut. No screams, shots or people came from the barn, so he turned to his phone and brought up the app.

The camera had landed almost against the wall, but it gave him a clear view of a small area encircled by farm equipment—and made his heart ache.

Sue sat on the floor with Drake, his dark head against her shoulder. Were they allowing her to say goodbye to her son before they tortured and killed her? Would they do the same to Drake?

A cold dread seeped into his veins as he thought about all the ways they could use Drake to get Sue to talk. But he was here now—watching everything they did.

Sue and Drake sat on the farthest side away from the door. A woman, he assumed Dani, and a man, who looked like Jeffrey, stood close to the door. They both had weapons, but they hung loosely in their hands. They figured their trusty guards would warn them of any trouble.

Hunter eyed the van with the dead man next to it, just feet from the front door. The construction of the barn wasn't very solid, and a heavy vehicle wouldn't have too much trouble crashing through that door.

Would Dani and Jeffrey react to the van's engine starting? Why wouldn't the guard start the van if he were cold and wanted the heat on? Would Sue realize what it meant? She had to know he had successfully tracked her and was planning her rescue.

Hunter shook his head and squeezed his eyes closed. Too much second-guessing. Too much indecision. Act. Move. Now.

He pushed away from the side of the barn and crawled toward the van. He stepped over the dead guy and settled behind the wheel, leaving the driver's door open. The keys in the ignition jiggled as his knee hit them.

He held his phone in front of him and propped it on top of the steering wheel. Dani and Jeffrey had their heads together, their guns at their sides. Sue had Drake in her lap. Good. Keep him safe.

He'd do the rest.

Without another thought clouding his brain or instinct, Hunter dropped the phone and replaced it with his weapon. In one movement, he cranked on the engine and stomped on the accelerator.

The van roared to life and barreled toward the barn door. As it crashed through and splintered the wood, he got a glimpse of Dani's face, eyes and mouth wide open. Jeffrey had rolled up onto the hood.

Hunter didn't relent, as he kept his foot firmly on the gas pedal. He heard a scream. A thud. A crunch.

He didn't hear any gunshots.

When the van reached the other side of the barn, Hunter bolted from the driver's seat. A twinge of fear brushed across the back of his neck when he didn't see Sue or Drake across the room where they'd been when he started his assault, but he had to neutralize the enemy first.

He kicked aside the debris and wreckage in the barn and stumbled upon Jeffrey, his crumpled body thrown up against some heavy machinery, his head at an odd angle. Hunter felt for a pulse—there was none.

As he turned from Jeffrey's dead body, he almost tripped over Dani's legs protruding from beneath the van's wheels. He crouched down, his gaze meeting her lifeless eyes, still wide-open. He growled, "And that's for my son."

"Hunter? Is it safe?"

Sue's voice calling out to him sent a rush of warm relief through his body, and for the first time that night, his rigid muscles lost a little of their tension.

He lurched to his feet and spotted her across the room, standing on a tractor, Drake clutched to her chest.

"It's safe. They're both dead."

They started toward each other at the same time, and for the first time, Hunter wrapped his arms around his son, safe in his mother's arms.

Epilogue

Ned dangled Sue's badge in front of her. "You're not out of the woods yet, Sue. Hunter took out several of Walid's cell here in DC, but we don't know how many are left and if they're going to be out for revenge."

As Sue hung her badge around her neck, she glanced at Hunter. "And we still don't know who the mole is—but we can all agree there is one."

Ned ran his finger along the seam of his lips. "The intel stays in this room…and with The Falcon's replacement."

"Who is?"

Hunter touched her hand. "I guess you'll never find out. You're off undercover duty."

"Your choice, right, Sue?" Ned raised his brows at her.

"Absolutely. I have a son to raise. Even my father's good with that."

"We've got plenty of analysis duty for you right here at home, but we're extending your leave for a little bit longer." He held up his hands. "For safety reasons only."

"That's fine. I need a break, and I know exactly where I'm going to take it."

Hunter extended his hand to Ned. "Thanks for guiding Sue through the process of coming out from under her undercover assignment."

"Once we got The Falcon's notes, it was easy." Ned crossed his arms. "Do you think you can get Major Denver to come in now?"

"I doubt it. He wants assurances before he surrenders, and the army is not ready to offer him those assurances yet."

"The Falcon made it clear that Denver's investigation was dovetailing with hers."

"Until the mole can be ID'd, I think Denver will remain in hiding."

Sue hitched her bag over her shoulder. "We'd better get going. Our son is with Peter right now and probably has him climbing the walls."

Sue and Hunter collected their son from her co-worker and exited the building, with Drake cuddled into Hunter's arms. After Hunter had saved them from the scary barn with the scary people, Drake had been clinging to his father as if he'd known him all his life.

They drove back to her place and Sue hesitated on the threshold. Her space, her life had been violated and the terrorists she'd been tracking for over three years were still out there…and Hunter had another deployment around the corner.

Hunter returned from his brief survey of her condo and nodded. "All clear."

Sue put Drake down and tousled his hair. "I think we should order pizza—one cheese and one with everything on it."

"Sounds good to me." Hunter patted his stomach.

Drake scampered to the packed suitcases in the corner of the room and tackled one. "Mama going?"

Sue's eyes stung and she sniffled through her smile. "You're coming with me this time, cupcake. I already told your aunt and cousins, and maybe they can visit us. We're going to Hunter's home in Colorado. He even has horses."

Drake skipped to Hunter and threw himself at his legs. "Horses."

Hunter scooped him up in his arms and flew him around the room a few times before settling on the sofa with him in his lap. Hunter touched his nose to Drake's. "You'd like a daddy, wouldn't you, Drake?"

Drake nodded and grabbed the buttons on Hunter's shirt. "Daddy."

Sue put a hand over her heart. It was as if he already knew.

"Well, I am your daddy. Is that okay? You can call me Daddy instead of Hunter. All right?"

Drake snuggled farther into Hunter's arms, burrowing against his chest. Still hanging on to the shirt button, he said, "Daddy."

"I guess that's settled." Hunter rested his chin on top of Drake's dark hair, a look of serene satisfaction softening the hard line of his jaw.

"And after Colorado? After your deployment?"

"I'm still gonna be Drake's dad…and your man, if you'll have me."

Sue meandered to the sofa where her two guys, her two heartbeats, cuddled together. She sank down next to Hunter and rested her head on his shoulder.

"If *I'll* have *you*? My concern is the other way around. I abandoned you. Lied to you. Kept your son from you and lied again."

"And I still love you. What does that say about me?" He pressed his lips against Drake's temple.

"That you're loyal and forgiving and a little bit crazy." She rubbed her knuckles against his chin. "You *did* crash headlong into a barn."

Dragging his fingers through her hair, he said, "My life was in that barn. My family. And I'm not gonna give up on my family—not now, not ever."

And just like that, Sue had her job, her man and her son back in her life.

* * * * *

Look for the next book in Carol Ericson's
Red, White and Built: Delta Force Deliverance,
Code Conspiracy, *available next month.*

And don't miss the previous book in the series:

Enemy Infiltration

Available now from Harlequin Intrigue!

WE HOPE YOU
ENJOYED THIS BOOK!

I N T R I G U E

Dive into action-packed suspense.
Solve crimes. Pursue justice.

Look for six new books available every
month, wherever books are sold!

AVAILABLE THIS MONTH FROM
Harlequin Intrigue®

SAFETY BREACH
Longview Ridge Ranch • by Delores Fossen
Former profiler Gemma Hanson is in witness protection, but she's still haunted by memories of the serial killer who tried to kill her last year. Her concerns skyrocket when Sheriff Kellan Slater tells her the murderer has learned her location and is coming to finish what he started.

UNDERCOVER ACCOMPLICE
Red, White and Built: Delta Force Deliverance
by Carol Ericson
When Delta Force soldier Hunter Mancini learns the group that kidnapped CIA operative Sue Chandler is now framing his team leader, he asks for her help. But could she be hiding something that would clear his boss?

AMBUSHED AT CHRISTMAS
Rushing Creek Crime Spree • by Barb Han
After a jogger resembling Detective Leah Cordon is murdered, rancher Deacon Kent approaches her, believing the attack is related to recent cattle mutilations. Can they find the killer before he corners Leah?

DANGEROUS CONDITIONS
Protectors at Heart • by Jenna Kernan
Former soldier Logan Lynch's first investigation as the constable of a small town leads him to microbiologist Paige Morris, whose boss was killed. Yet as they search for the murderer, Paige is forced to reveal a secret that shows the stakes couldn't be higher.

RULES IN DEFIANCE
Blackhawk Security • by Nichole Severn
Blackhawk Security investigator Elliot Dunham never expected his neighbor to show up bruised and covered in blood in the middle of the night. To protect Waylynn Hargraves, Elliot must defy the rules he's set for himself, because he knows he's all that stands between her and certain death.

HIDDEN TRUTH
Stealth • by Danica Winters
When undercover CIA agent Trevor Martin meets Sabrina Parker, the housekeeper at the ranch where he's lying low, he doesn't know she's an undercover FBI agent. After a murder on the property, the operatives must work together, but can they discover their hidden connection before it's too late?

HIATMBPA1219

Get 4 FREE REWARDS!

We'll send you 2 FREE Books <u>plus</u> 2 FREE Mystery Gifts.

Harlequin Intrigue® books feature heroes and heroines that confront and survive danger while finding themselves irresistibly drawn to one another.

FREE Value Over **$20**

Love Harlequin romance?

DISCOVER.

Be the first to find out about promotions,
news and exclusive content!

Facebook.com/HarlequinBooks

Twitter.com/HarlequinBooks

Instagram.com/HarlequinBooks

Pinterest.com/HarlequinBooks

ReaderService.com

EXPLORE.

Sign up for the Harlequin e-newsletter and
download a free book from any series at
TryHarlequin.com.

CONNECT.

Join our Harlequin community to share
your thoughts and connect with other
romance readers!
Facebook.com/groups/HarlequinConnection

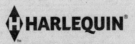

HARLEQUIN®

**ROMANCE WHEN
YOU NEED IT**

HSOCIAL2018